"You look really hot, voice husky

"And how." Deanie turned and squinted up at his large shadow towering over her. "There were no umbrellas available, and so I've been cooking."

He grinned. "I meant hot as in good-looking." Before she could answer him, he'd hooked a leg over the chair and straddled the chaise behind her. His thighs framed hers and his chest cushioned her back. His hands settled on her shoulders, then traced her upper arms. Deanie could barely breathe.

"You feel hot, too," he added, his lips touching the shell of her ear.

"It's the sun," she said weakly.

"Maybe." His hands slid back up over her shoulders. "And maybe not." Strong fingers lifted her hair away from her neck and she felt the cool rush of fresh air followed by the hot press of his lips.

"What are you doing?"

"Following the Camp E.D.E.N. curriculum and the first workshop—'Shedding Your Inhibitions.'"

"Shouldn't we find someplace a little more private? With less people?"

"Now, Deanie," Rance said, grinning wickedly. "Wouldn't that defeat the whole purpose?"

Blaze™

Dear Reader,

Being a romantic at heart, I love Valentine's Day. It's an infatuation that began long before I met my husband and fell in love. Lucky for him. See, my hubby is a total nonromantic. His last V-Day gift to me? A fishing rod and reel combo from the local sporting goods store. But for me, it's not the actual gifts that make Valentine's Day so special. It's the whole notion of an entire twenty-four hours devoted to the big *L*. It's just so… romantic.

But I have a lot of friends—single women, as well as married ones—who think I'm a nutcase. They hate the cheesy cards and the never-ending pressure that comes with a holiday where the depth of a person's love is often measured by the size of the gift.

Like my gal pals, Deanie Codge, the heroine in my newest Harlequin Blaze novel, is totally convinced that Valentine's Day is *the* worst day of the year. Not because she doesn't enjoy a box of Godiva, mind you, but because she simply doesn't believe in love. She's been there and done that, and she's *not* doing it again.

But when she finds herself stranded on a romantic island for twenty-four hours with her old flame, Rance McGraw, she starts to think that maybe, *just maybe* falling in love again might not be all that bad. After all, it *is* Valentine's Day….

Join Deanie and Rance as they spend their hottest holiday ever in *Tall, Tanned & Texan,* and have a blazing-hot Valentine's Day!

Kimberly Raye

P.S. I love to hear from readers! You can visit me online at www.kimberlyraye.com or write to me c/o Harlequin Books.

KIMBERLY RAYE
Tall, Tanned & Texan

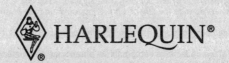

TORONTO • NEW YORK • LONDON
AMSTERDAM • PARIS • SYDNEY • HAMBURG
STOCKHOLM • ATHENS • TOKYO • MILAN • MADRID
PRAGUE • WARSAW • BUDAPEST • AUCKLAND

This book is dedicated to the
wonderfully talented Nina Bangs.
Thanks for being such a great writer
and an even better friend!

ISBN 0-373-79237-9

TALL, TANNED & TEXAN

www.eHarlequin.com

Printed in U.S.A.

1

DEANIE CODGE had been waiting her entire adult life to experience really great sex.

Sex that included lots of slow, deep kisses and long, lingering touches. Sex that stole her breath away and zapped her common sense. Sex that made her toes tingle and her skin prickle and her body actually *throb*.

Sex that didn't involve a sleeping bag, a can of insect repellant and the bed of a beat-up pickup truck.

Now, after twenty-nine years and one too many mosquito bites, she was *this* close.

Deanie stowed her purse beneath the seat in front of her and her hand paused on the side pocket where she'd tucked her cell phone. She slid it free and noted the flashing message light before powering it off. She had five messages. Probably one from each of her older brothers. Or maybe they were all from Clay. He wasn't the oldest, but he was the only one who'd settled down and found the right woman. His wife, Helen, was pregnant with their first child, which was due any day now. Since Clay had taken over the family's cattle ranch—their father suffered from rheumatoid arthritis and had handed over the workload to his most responsible son and the only one who'd stuck around Romeo—he now considered himself the head of the family. While their dad spent his time playing bingo and gossiping down at the Fat Cow Diner, Clay kept track of ten thousand cattle and his baby sister. She could only imagine the fit he was throwing after discovering that she was missing in action.

Technically, she wasn't *missing*. She'd left a letter clearly explaining what she was doing. At the same time, while the letter was meant to inform, she knew its contents would make her overprotective brother worry that much more.

It wasn't every day that his baby sister signed up for boot camp.

A *sexual* boot camp, that is.

She ignored the small spiral of guilt, stowed her cell phone and fastened her seat belt. She lifted the oval window shade and stared at the hustle and bustle. Beyond the glass, she could see the white and gray building that housed the terminals for

San Antonio International Airport. A cart overflowing with luggage, her new white and pink flowered canvas bags balanced on top, rolled toward the turquoise-and-white 747. The gray tunnel she'd just walked through still sat attached to the doorway of the plane. The last few passengers filed inside, twisting this way and that to make it down the narrow aisle that separated pairs of seats.

Excitement zipped up her spine and her hands trembled. This was *it*. The second step in transforming her ho-hum, going-absolutely-nowhere life.

The first had involved the purchase of the pair of three inch stilettos currently cutting off the blood supply to her toes and the cotton sundress that clung to her as if it were hanging on for dear life.

She drew a deep breath and tried to ignore the way her chest pressed against the low-cut halter top.

So what if it was skimpy? And pink? It was feminine. Trendy. *Sexy.* There would be no mistaking Deanie Codge for one of the boys in this get-up.

She looked one hundred percent female.

As for feeling like one… Okay, so it wasn't quite happening.

Yet.

Growing up the youngest of five brothers, she hadn't had much of an opportunity to explore her feminine side. Her mother had passed away right after giving birth to Deanie, and so she'd been raised by her father and brothers on a small cattle ranch in the middle of Nowhere, Texas aka Romeo.

It had been survival of the fittest in the Codge household, complete with wrestling matches to determine who used the bathroom first and shooting competitions to decide who did what chores. Being the youngest and the smallest, she'd ended up pitching hay and cleaning out stalls more times than she could count. She'd also been extremely lucky to get a full five minutes in front of the mirror every morning. Not nearly enough time to primp her way to womanhood, even if she'd wanted to. Overall, she'd grown up feeling like one of the boys.

Oddly enough, it had never really bothered her. Deanie had always been happy with herself. Content.

Until six weeks ago when Harwin Mulligan—the low-down, sneaky rat bastard—had stolen her promotion *and* cheated on her with Dora Mae Shriver.

She'd realized then and there that she would never be taken seriously as a mechanic. While her customers—namely the entire Senior Women's Rotary Club—trusted her with their Cadillacs and Bonnevilles, Big Daddy, the owner of Romeo's largest auto shop where she'd worked for the past ten years, obviously did not. Otherwise, he would never have left his brake specialist—aka Harwin aka the low-down, sneaky rat bastard—in charge while he raced off to Mexico on a fishing trip.

She'd known then that if Big Daddy wouldn't let her run Big Daddy's Auto & Body for a measly six week vacation, he certainly wouldn't let her take over the place when he officially retired. It didn't matter that she was the best mechanic in town or that she'd worked her way through the local junior college and earned an associates degree in business.

Her dreams of managing the auto shop and building up the business while saving to eventually buy out Big Daddy had died as fast as the old, souped up Toyota pickup she'd driven her senior year of high school. It wasn't going to happen.

Not now.

Not ever.

As had the crazy, insane notion that she was going to ever meet *the* man. A man who would know a few things about romance. A man who wouldn't assume she didn't give a lick about those things just because she didn't look all soft and frilly and *girlie*. A man who could give her the best, most amazing orgasm of her life. A man who would love her and not so much as glance at Dora Mae or any of the other hotties down at the Fat Cow Diner.

A man who would see beneath her rough-and-tough exterior to the heart and soul of the woman who lay beneath.

Yeah, right.

It seemed her overalls were made of Kryptonite because no man had ever seen beyond the surface. Except Harwin, or so she'd thought. But then he'd stolen Big Daddy's confidence and gone after someone prettier, more feminine and a zillion times better in bed.

Deanie would never forget Dora in her red thong and matching bra, a large red feather in her hand as she leaned over Harwin, who'd been spread-eagled and tied to the bed with a pair of fuzzy red handcuffs.

In her wildest dreams, Deanie could never have cooked up such a scene. A fact that spoke volumes for her sexual know-how. Or lack thereof.

Determination flowed through her. She ignored her pinched toes and the goose bumps chasing up and down her arms thanks to the revealing sundress. It was time for something drastic. A change.

An extreme makeover.

Deanie had started with the outside. She'd left her dead-end job, spruced up her blah hairstyle, re-vamped her vampless wardrobe.

Now she was ready to tackle the inside.

She leaned over, reached into her purse and pulled out a folded brochure.

Two weeks to a new and improved, sexier you!

The main caption leaped out at her and she grasped at the hope that blossomed in her chest.

In exactly three hours, after stopping in Miami to pick up more passengers and a thirty minute layover on a neighboring island, Deanie would arrive in Eden, a small island in the heart of the Caribbean and home to Camp E.D.E.N. The honest-to-goodness sexual boot camp helped individuals nurture their sexuality. Their specialty was an intensive fourteen day training program that included everything from an anatomy class called Treasure Island 101: If You Can't Find It, You Can't Use It, to Cooking To Cuddle: The Best Aphrodisiac Foods.

By the time Deanie graduated from Camp E.D.E.N., she would be more than ready to begin a new life in Dallas, complete with an apartment in the heart of the city and a job as manager of Sweet Nothings, an upscale lingerie boutique owned by one of her mother's old high school friends. Miss MaryBelle had been surprised and happy to hear from Deanie. She and Deanie's mother had been close and so she'd been more than willing to consider Deanie's résumé.

Consider, mind you.

Miss MaryBelle was a businesswoman first and so she'd been clear about the fact that she couldn't give Deanie a job just because she and Deanie's mother had giggled about boys in the girls' bathroom all four years of high school. Business was business.

Thankfully.

Where Big Daddy had been more influenced by a set of balls—and not very big ones—rather than an associates degree, Miss MaryBelle didn't subscribe to the good ole boys' club. The old woman had been impressed enough to start Deanie off as a manager-in-training. Now it was adios to her life as a small-town mechanic and, especially, her reputation as Romeo's resident tomboy.

A change she never could have made if she'd stayed put. While the town itself had changed over the years, the people hadn't. The Piggly Wiggly had added a self checkout lane, but the owner, Mr. McGhee still bagged up everyone's groceries himself. Moe's Gas Station had turned into a self-serve with pay-at-the-pump options, but Mr. Johnson, the clerk, still rushed out to wash everyone's windshield and share the latest gossip. The old rodeo arena where Deanie had spent her weekends watching Clay and his best friend,

Rance McGraw wrestle steers was just weeks away from being bulldozed to make way for one of those superstores, but Mr. Samuels, the grounds-keeper, still raked the arena dirt every afternoon the way he'd been doing for the past twenty years.

The folks in her hometown would never see her as anything other than the tomboy she'd always been.

She ignored the pang of regret in the pit of her stomach and checked her watch. Even though they were already five minutes past takeoff, she should still arrive on the island in plenty of time to make the camp's afternoon check-in.

Most of the passengers had already boarded and so the flight attendant started down the center aisle, checking the overhead compartments and closing the bins.

Deanie had just stuffed the brochure back into her purse and settled into her seat when she heard the soft, sugary voice.

"Coming through, hon."

A heartbeat later, a tall woman folded herself into the seat next to Deanie's.

"Thank God for flight delays," the twentysome-thing woman exclaimed. She had long blond curls brushed out just enough to make them full and wild. Streaks of platinum added to the overall effect.

She wore a stretchy blue top, the neck outlined with sequins and matching beads. A short blue skirt clung to her hips and rode high on her thighs as she adjusted herself on the seat. Her legs were long and tanned and bare. Her feet disappeared into a pair of three-inch blue sandals even higher than the shoes Deanie wore. A matching clutch purse sat in her lap. French-manicured fingertips reached for the edges of the seat belt.

"Now," she declared as the buckle clicked into place. "I can actually breathe. For a few minutes there, I didn't think I was going to make it." Her hot pink lips parted in a smile as she turned blue eyes the same color as her outfit on Deanie. "I couldn't get Roger off the cell phone. I swear, he's this close to being a Fatal Attraction, you know what I mean?"

"Boy, do I ever." The comment came from the seat in front of Deanie. A heartbeat later, a large, red beehive hairdo pushed into view, followed by the thin, narrow face of a fiftyish woman. She wore flaming orange lipstick and a pair of gold-framed glasses that looked two sizes too big for her thin face. Her cheeks were pinked with too much rouge and bright blue eye shadow clung to her lids. She smelled of hair spray, old perfume and mothballs.

"You try to let them off easy," the woman continued, "but they just can't take no for an answer. They keep calling and showing up and sending flowers and buying jewelry. I can't be bought, I've said more times than I can count." She made a face that deepened the wrinkles around her eyes. "But that still didn't stop Walter from sending over that Rolls Royce last month."

"A man bought you a Rolls Royce?" the twenty-something asked, a look of disbelief on her face.

"He tried, but I'm still partial to the Porsche that James gave me for my birthday last year. James..." She sighed. "Now there was a man who had good taste. Unfortunately, he had a bad colon. Keeled over during dinner a few months later and that was that. It's always the good ones that go young. Remember that, child," she told Deanie. "If you find a grade A, quality man, you latch on to him fast and don't waste a moment, especially if there's a nasty colon involved."

"Words to live by," the blonde murmured.

"And how, otherwise I would be home watching my soap operas right now instead of popping Dramamine." At Deanie's questioning expression, she added, "Men usually fly to me, mind you, not the other way around. Then again, Mitchell isn't your typical man. Why, he actually wrote me a love poem, of all things. I couldn't very well let him abandon a million-dollar deal just to fly to Texas to see me for Valentine's Day after that. Not that he needs the money. He's got the stuff coming out his ears."

"You've got a millionaire writing you love poems?" The blonde sounded as skeptical as she looked.

The redheaded woman didn't seem the least put out. "Actually, he's a billionaire. And he's handsome. And a good dancer. And a great bingo player. Not that any of that means anything. Why, I've known handsome, bingo-playing, tangoing billionaires before, but none of them knew how to appreciate the real me. The personality beneath the decorative package." She patted her hairdo with a bony hand. "Mavoreen Rosenbaum does have a brain, too. Unfortunately, men are simple creatures much too caught up in their hormones to understand that."

At that moment, a man bolted through the doorway and started down the aisle. He wore a three-piece suit and a haggard expression. He rushed past Deanie's aisle, only to stop and retrace his steps until he stood next to Mavoreen Rosenbaum. He pointed his briefcase at the empty seat beside her. "I'm sitting there."

"Of course you are," she told him. "What can I say?" Mavoreen shook her head. "I guess we all have our crosses to bear." She turned to let the man scoot past her. "I'll expect you to keep your hands to yourself," she told him as he settled in. "And your legs. And all other body parts. And don't even think about staring at me, sonny, because I've got a stun gun in my purse and I know how to use it…"

"If she's got a decorative package, I'm Shrek," the blonde murmured.

As far out as the notion seemed, Deanie couldn't help but admire the older woman. "At least she's confident."

"She's delusional. There is no billionaire. It's just a story she makes up so she doesn't have to look like a lonely desperate woman, which is what she is." The blonde smiled. "But enough with the small stuff. I'm Savannah Sierra Ellington."

"Nadine. Nadine Codge. But you can call me Deanie."

The woman's smile widened and she winked. "Thank the good Lord for flight delays *and* nicknames."

Before they could exchange any more pleasantries, the flight attendant's voice carried over the loud speaker.

Deanie shifted her attention to the woman wearing the white blouse trimmed in turquoise piping and khaki slacks, and did her best not to grimace.

A reaction that had nothing to do with the fact that she was on an airplane for the first time in her life. Or that it just so happened to be Friday the thirteenth. No it was the cupid cutouts and heart streamers that decorated the front of the plane in honor of tomorrow.

V-Day.

The worst day of any single girl's life.

The flight attendant wore a flashing neon heart pin. A red scarf dotted with red lips circled her neck. To top off her tribute to the big L, she sported a headband with a pair of red glitter hearts attached via long, tentacle-looking wires. The hearts bobbed with her every movement.

"…a little delay, but while we're waiting for the tower to give the go-ahead for takeoff, we'll start our in-flight service by taking drink orders." She started down the aisle, pen and paper in hand. In her wake, another flight attendant carried a large red bag filled with packages of pretzels. She passed out the goodies and carefully eyeballed everyone's seat belt.

"Welcome to Island Airways where love is

always in the air," the flight attendant with the pretzels told them after her partner had taken their drink orders.

"This is too much," Savannah Ellington exclaimed when the attendants had moved to the next row.

"You said it." Even the pretzel bags were red with tiny silver hearts. Deanie fought back the memory that pushed its way into her head… Of a hopeful young girl, a shoe box full of homemade sugar cookies and the most handsome boy in the seventh grade.

She'd been so silly back then and Mr. Handsome hadn't been the least bit interested. Not that she'd taken the hint. She'd made more sugar cookies the next year and the next, and the only thing he'd ever given her in return had been a thank-you and a grin.

Ah, but that grin had been worth the entire day spent in the kitchen and her brothers' teasing.

At least that's what she'd thought back then. But then she'd wised up.

Sure, you did. After you made an even bigger fool of yourself.

"I'm definitely going to complain to the higher ups," Savannah said. "This just isn't right."

"I know. It's not like it's a *major* holiday. We're

not talking Christmas, for Pete's sake. It's just Valentine's Day."

"I wasn't talking about Valentine's Day." Savannah held up the red foil bag. "*One* serving? Talk about chintzy. Forget dancing the night away once I get to Escapades. I'll be too weak from lack of proper nutrition." She dropped the bag into her lap and unlatched her purse. A little digging and she withdrew a candy bar. "Thank God I think ahead." She tore the wrapper, broke a piece of candy off and popped it into her mouth. Her expression eased as she savored the mouthful before holding the bar out to Deanie. "Want some?"

Deanie shook her head.

Savannah gave her a knowing look. "It figures."

"What?"

"If you hate Valentine's Day, you're bound to hate candy, too. And flowers. And jewelry."

"I don't *hate* Valentine's Day. I just think it's a little overdone." And depressing. "People shouldn't have to buy candy or flowers or jewelry to prove their love."

"Says you." She ate another piece of candy and eyed Deanie. "You don't have a boyfriend, do you?"

"Not exactly."

"Not exactly no, or not exactly yes?"

Deanie swallowed. "We broke up."

Savannah studied her a few more seconds before winking. "Don't sweat it. There are plenty more where he came from. Real ones," she added, nodding toward Mavoreen's beehive that bobbed above the seat in front of her. "And trust me, the more the merrier. That way when one's busy in Atlanta with a buyout for his precious company, you don't have to sit around feeling sorry for yourself. You just hop a plane to a tropical paradise and party the night away with boyfriend number two. And number three. And number four. It's all about having a back-up plan."

For the lucky few like Savannah Sierra Ellington with her feminine clothes and her breathy voice. She practically oozed sex appeal. It made sense that she would snag more than one man's attention.

Deanie, on the other hand, wasn't as concerned with snagging every man's attention as she was with keeping one man's attention.

The man.

And so she intended to be ready when he happened along.

If he happened along.

"I shouldn't have had that extra glass of wine in the airport lounge. I think I'll head to the ladies' room before we takeoff." Savannah tucked the remainder of her candy bar into her purse, popped open her seat belt, pushed to her feet and sashayed the few feet to the lavatory at the front of the plane.

Deanie glanced at her watch again. Anxiety rushed through her, chasing away the excitement. They really needed to get going. The last thing she wanted was to be late.

Camp E.D.E.N. ran a tight ship. There would be no lounging around the pool or writing post cards. Her training would start immediately after check-in with the first workshop—Shedding Your Inhibitions. There would be a thirty minute dinner break and then it was back to work with three more workshops before curfew and lights out. The strict regimen went hand-in-hand with the camp's no-nonsense image. Camp E.D.E.N. was for the serious, self-improvement-minded individual, not the fun-seeking sort. At least that's what the Web site and its page of testimonials claimed.

Her toes whimpered and she eased her feet out of her shoes just enough to allow some breathing room. She shifted and tried for a more comfortable position. The seat was more narrow than she'd initially thought, her legs a lot more cramped. Jet-setting to a tropical getaway wasn't at all as glamorous as she'd imagined.

It felt more like being cooped up in the last row

of a school bus with the other equipment assistants—all three of them, Deanie included—while the football players rode up front.

Then again, this wasn't high school.

This was her life.

The new and improved version.

"This is a good day." She murmured the words her grandmother had recited to her every morning during her summer visits before the old woman had passed away.

A great day.

A scary day.

She forced aside the last thought.

Exciting, not scary.

Of course, both caused massive bursts of adrenaline and a faint, light-headed feeling so it was understandable how she could confuse the two.

She pulled out the latest fashion magazine she'd bought at the newsstand—after reaching for *Sports Illustrated* and giving herself a mental hand slap—and flipped to an article that debated the benefits of lip gloss versus lipstick. Then she heard something…

It took her all of two seconds to realize it wasn't just the cramped space that reminded her of her high school days.

It was the deep, husky voice that slid into her ears.

"…wouldn't say I was the *greatest* tackle to ever play pro football. Maybe one of the top five…"

It couldn't be.

Deanie closed her eyes for a long moment, her heart beating frantically, as the past pushed and pulled at her.

"Hey there, Teeny."

The familiar voice echoed in her memory and she practically smelled the sharp aroma of cattle and hay that had filled the corral where she'd watched her brother and his best friend practice steer wrestling techniques every afternoon after school.

"…I managed to hold my own, but there were a lot of players just as good…"

She forced her eyes open, drew a deep breath and twisted to peer over the top of her seat.

Rance McGraw had been the hottest, hunkiest boy to ever wear a Romeo High School football jersey. He'd been the youngest and the wildest of the notorious McGraw triplets, the star of Deanie's adolescent fantasies and a few adult ones, as well. He'd been sweet and charming and charismatic, and one of the best steer wrestlers to ever win first place at Romeo Junior Livestock Show and Rodeo. He'd also been the boy Deanie had wanted desperately to marry and live happily ever after with.

Wanted, as in past tense. She'd given up her infatuation with him a long time ago.

Sixteen years was a long time, however, and the boy had turned into a hotter, hunkier man.

The man now sitting two rows behind her.

She swallowed and tried for a deep breath. But while her brain issued the command, her lungs wouldn't cooperate. Neither would her eyes. She willed them to look away, but they kept staring, drinking in the picture he made, his tall, muscular form barely contained in the narrow seat.

With his dark hair and *good ole boy* smile, Rance was the spitting image of his two handsome brothers. He had the same strong jaw, sensuous lips and sculpted nose. At the same time, there would be no mistaking him for the other two. Being a fraternal triplet, he didn't have blue eyes like Mason or green ones like Josh. Rather, his gaze gleamed as bright, as bold, as intoxicating as a shot of Jack Daniels whiskey.

Even more, Rance had his own style that set him apart. He wasn't the classic clean-cut cowboy type like the other McGraw men. Rather, his dark hair hung down to his shoulders. He wore a bright Hawaiian print shirt unbuttoned, a white NASCAR T-shirt beneath. She couldn't see without giving herself whiplash, but she'd be willing to bet that he wore his signature board shorts, long and frayed around the edges, and a pair of flip-flops.

The only indication of his cowboy roots was the beat-up straw Resistol that he'd been wearing since the age of sixteen. It had belonged to his father who'd died that year. The hat looked worn and faded now, a Coors Lite patch stitched to the brim in between a patch for last year's ESPN Extreme Sports Games in Colorado and another advertising the bungee jumping finals in South America.

The media still referred to him as a cowboy, however, because of his do-anything attitude and I-don't-give-a-damn appearance. Rance was an ex-pro football player who now owned a chain of extreme sporting good stores and still made the news with his passion for the outrageous. Just last year she'd seen him on TV hang gliding over a sea of hungry sharks.

Crazy.

Not Rance, mind you. She understood his competitive drive better than anyone because she knew the circumstance behind it. His parents had died when he'd been sixteen, and a little of his heart had died with them. He'd been trying to revive it ever since with a constant supply of adrenaline rush.

No, Deanie was the crazy one.

Her heart pounded. Her vision blurred. Her hands even trembled.

And all because of the fact that Rance McGraw was *this* close and, despite every argument to the contrary, Deanie still wanted him more than her next breath.

She didn't know whether to crawl across the seat and kiss him for all she was worth, or kick his ass sixty ways to Sunday.

On the one hand, she'd vowed to abandon her hellion ways and conduct herself in a more ladylike fashion from here on out.

On the other hand, she'd offered herself to Rance once before and it had gotten her the ultimate rejection.

She weighed the two options for several frantic heartbeats.

Better to go with plan B.

Deanie unfastened her seat belt and pushed to her feet.

2

WHEN IT CAME TO WOMEN, Rance McGraw had never been a man to turn tail and run the other way.

He liked women. Hell, he loved 'em and he wasn't the least bit shy about it.

He loved the silky feel of a woman's hair trailing between his fingers. The softness of her skin against his lips during a deep, hot kiss. The rasp of her nails up and down his back as he plunged deep inside her body. The soft, sweet, breathless sound of her voice as she begged for more…

Yep, he loved women, all right. As thoroughly and as often as possible. And they loved him.

Deanie Codge, in particular.

She'd been head over heels for him since the day he'd paired up with her brother, Clay, for the annual steer wrestling competition.

Rance had been eight years old when he'd gone home with Clay to practice. Deanie had been four, and hell-bent on joining in the wrestling match.

When Clay had captured her in a headlock to teach her a lesson and force her to leave them alone, Rance had gone to her rescue.

It was the biggest mistake of his life.

Free of her brother's hold, Deanie had stared up at him with wide, adoring blue eyes, and the damage had been done. She'd followed him around from then on, clear up until the night he'd graduated high school and left for college.

A vision pulled him back and he saw her standing on the grassy bank of McGraw River, her long, dark hair hanging down around her shoulders, her pale, naked body shimmering in the moonlight.

He didn't remember much about that night except that he'd started out at Dorie Jackson's graduation party with his buddies and a keg of beer. He wasn't sure exactly how he made it out to the creek or what happened to the dozen or so guys he'd been party-hopping with. The evening was just a blur up until that moment when he found himself alone on the riverbank with Deanie.

His senses had sharpened then and he'd drank in the sight of her, from the faint stirring of her hair to the goose bumps that had chased up and down her pale arms, to the pucker of her ripe, rosy nipples. He'd heard the slight gurgle of water where it fed from the underground spring, the buzz of crickets and the thunder of his own heartbeat. He'd smelled the vanilla and sugar scent of her Sweet Honesty perfume. He'd tasted the surprise on his own tongue and he'd felt the sharp tightening of his groin.

That had been the first time he'd ever seen her naked. And the last.

Hell, that had been the last time he'd seen her, period. He'd been back in Romeo only a handful of times over the past sixteen years and he'd always made it his business to steer clear of Deanie Codge.

He'd succeeded up until a few months ago when he'd come face-to-face with her at the double wedding of his older brothers, Josh and Mason. Rance was the third and youngest of the McGraw triplets, and the only remaining bachelor. A title he intended to keep for as long as possible. His living-on-the-edge lifestyle wasn't conducive to a long-term relationship and so he'd avoided them.

Much the same way he'd avoided Deanie.

She'd caught up with him, however, and confirmed what he'd started to suspect months before, when he'd come home to mend after breaking his leg en route to an alligator wrestling competition in Australia. Namely that she no longer carried a torch for him.

As owner and spokesperson for Extreme Dream, the South's largest chain of extreme sporting goods stores, Rance competed in everything from snowboarding to offtrack dirt bikes. He'd skiied down the Riviera, base-jumped off the Empire State Building and parasailed over piranha-infested waters off the coast of Thailand.

Scary stuff, but not half as frightening as meeting up with Deanie, and so Rance had kept his return a secret from any and everyone.

At least he'd tried.

But then a sudden craving for something sweet had forced him to make a midnight run to the local diner. Word had traveled in the time it had taken to eat one slice of Miss Mona's unforgettable cherry pie and he'd been screwed.

Or so he'd thought.

But in the days that had followed, Deanie had made no attempt to contact him.

Until the wedding.

She'd spotted him and he'd spotted her. They'd exchanged the usual pleasantries. And then…

Nada.

No stealing glances at him during the ceremony. No bugging him to dance at the reception. No following him home with his favorite pepperoni and jalapeno pizza. No showing up on his doorstep with his favorite silver dollar blue-berry pancakes the next morning. No inviting him to the local Friday night football game or Saturday bingo or Sunday morning church.

That had been a week ago. The longest week of his life. He hadn't slept. He'd barely eaten. He'd spent his time thinking. Worrying. Wondering. What the hell had happened?

Suddenly, his gaze collided with a pair of sizzling blue eyes fringed in dark black lashes. Her eyebrows were drawn together, her full, pink lips pulled into a tight frown. Her shoulders were rigid, her move-ments stiff as she sidestepped in front of the seat next to her and stepped purposely into the aisle.

She looked ready to explode, and not in an or-gasmically good way.

That's it, buddy. She's over you. And once she gets in touch with her sexuality at Camp E.D.E.N., she'll be on to bigger and better things and she'll really *be over you.*

His gut tightened and it took all of his effort to keep the smile on his face from hardening into a frown. So she wasn't tagging along after him like she used to? It didn't mean she wasn't still wildly attracted to him.

She still wanted him, all right.

He knew it. He felt it.

Even if she was doing a damned fine job of hiding it.

Remember your objective—intercept and turnaround.

While Deanie had every right to lead her own life the way she saw fit, her older brothers felt differently, particularly Rance's longtime friend and best bud, Clay. The man was frantic. Not because his baby sister couldn't make her own decisions and switch jobs, or even cities, if she felt like it.

But enrolling in a *sex* camp?

Clay had been ready to follow her himself, despite the fact that he was going to be a father any minute. But then Rance had shown up and volunteered for the job.

"You don't have time for this."

He could still hear Shank Murphy when Rance had dialed him up en route to the airport. Shank was the chief marketing director for Extreme Dream and Rance's business partner. He'd had a fit when Rance had told him that he wouldn't be flying back to Austin today because he had to do a favor for an old friend.

"You have to come back today. You've got to pick up your gear and catch a plane tomorrow in order to make personal appearances for the upcoming competition."

*"Pack and ship my gear and I'll pick it up when
I get there."*

*"Tomorrow. You have to leave tomorrow. I don't
care where you are or what you're doing."*

"I'll be there."

Which meant he had twenty-four hours to talk
some sense into one very stubborn Deanie Codge.

He'd wanted to sling her over his shoulder and
haul her off the plane the moment he'd set eyes on
her, but that would have just made her mad. He
didn't want her mad. Mad meant stubborn, which
meant she would do anything just to spite him. In-
cluding booking herself on the next flight out the
minute his back was turned. No, he wanted her
stuck so that she would have no choice but to
listen to reason.

A *sex* camp, of all things. While the setup had
looked respectable enough when he and Clay had
looked it up on the Internet, Rance could only
imagine what really went on at a place like that.

In fact, he'd spent the better part of the cab ride
to the airport imagining it, and so he'd been pretty
worked up before he'd seen her board the plane in
her skimpy dress and do-me high heels.

Seeing her up close and personal, smelling the
sweet sent of vanilla and sugar that still clung to
her, hearing the slight breathlessness in her voice

when she spoke worked him up even more. He knew then as he stared up at her that he wasn't just here because of his friendship with Clay.

Deanie had been the one constant in his life. The one person he could count on to always be there. The one person who'd really liked him. The one person who'd cared.

The only person.

She couldn't *not* be attracted to him anymore.

Particularly since he was about to bust his pants at the sight of her.

He tamped down his lust, shifted in his seat and put on his game face.

"Hey, there, Teeny." He grinned when she reached him. "Fancy meeting you here."

She glared down at him. "I'm going to kill you. First I'm going to shoot you, then I'm going to skin your sorry hide, and *then* I'm going to hang what's left for the buzzards."

"Careful with the sweet talk." He winked. "Otherwise, I'm liable to think you've still got the hots for me."

Her eyes softened and he knew then that she wasn't as immune to him as she pretended to be. But then her expression hardened again. "In your dreams."

He grinned, slow and sure. "Amen."

AMEN?

As in he actually dreamed about her?

Deanie entertained the possibility for several fast, furious heartbeats before reminding herself that this was Rance McGraw.

As in the Rance McGraw who'd never so much as glanced her way romantically while growing up.

As in *the* Rance McGraw who'd turned her down cold the night she'd offered her body to him.

"I can't do it," he'd told her.

Unfortunately, rumor said he'd done *it* with every cheerleader who'd shaken a pair of pom-poms his way and so Deanie knew that it wasn't so much the fact that he couldn't do it, but that he couldn't do it with her.

Or rather, he *wouldn't*.

Because Deanie hadn't been a cheerleader. Or a twirler. Or even a pep squad member. Heck, she hadn't been a member of anything except the auto shop club and she'd only joined that because her brother, Clay, had served as president to earn extra credit in shop class. He'd promised to rally for the club and boost its membership, and so he'd re-cruited his best friend, Rance, to help him. That had been enough incentive for Deanie and she'd gladly forked over two dollars in dues and worked her buns off to help Clay pass his senior elective.

Clay.

The name stuck in her head and Rance's sudden appearance started to make sense. Her brother had a wife who was nine months pregnant. He couldn't come running after her. So he'd asked his oldest friend to do it for him.

"Clay put you up to this, didn't he?" she asked with tight lips.

"Up to what?"

"This." She gestured around. "You're following me."

"You're the one who came to me, Teeny. I don't recall jumping out of my seat to walk over to you."

"You know what I mean."

He gave her a wide-eyed look that might have hinted at innocence if the Devil himself hadn't danced in the bright gold depths of his eyes. "I don't have a clue."

"Okay, if you're not following me, then what *are* you doing?"

He held up a bag of pretzels. "Just having a damned fine snack, darlin'."

She ignored the shiver that rippled through her at the endearment. "I mean, what are you doing on this plane? On this flight?"

He winked. "I'm on my way to camp."

"*You're* going to Camp E.D.E.N.?"

"Sure am."

"But why? It's a…" The word *sex* stalled on the tip of her tongue and her mouth went dry. She swallowed. "It's not the sort of place you would want to go."

"Actually, I think it's exactly the sort of place I'd want to go."

"Why? Because you need sex lessons?"

"I was thinking I could give a few."

"You're going as an instructor?"

He must have read the disbelief in her voice because his grin faltered just a little. "I'm truly hurt, Teeny, that you don't think I have anything to offer by way of sexual expertise." He stared up at her, into her, and his gaze added, *I seem to recall a time when you felt completely different.*

"You already have a job," she said, eager to ignore the sudden memory that rushed at her. Of a moonlit creek bank and a desperately hopeful girl and… Uh, uh. She wasn't going there.

Not now. Not ever again.

"This is just a little side project to break the monotony. I need some variety in my life."

"You're an extreme sports fanatic. Your life is nothing but variety."

"Too much of anything can become routine." He winked. "Say, maybe you'll end up in one of my classes."

It took everything she had not to give in to the sudden shiver that raced through her at the prospect.

First off, if he were an actual instructor, she wouldn't get lucky enough to wind up in his class. Second, she knew full well that Camp E.D.E.N. only employed educated professionals. While Rance had the experience and know-how, he didn't have a Ph.D. in sex education. Which meant he'd cooked up the story to cover the real reason for his presence.

Clay.

She planted her hands on her hips. "If Clay thinks I'm going to change my mind just because you're here, he can think again. I'm going to Eden."

"Then so am I." He grinned. "After all, duty calls."

SHE SHOULD HAVE KNOWN better than to leave a note.

Deanie spent the entire trip to Miami mentally kicking her own ass for being so stupid. But she hadn't wanted Clay to worry. Unfortunately, she hadn't wanted to lie to him, either, and so she was stuck with Rance for the entire flight.

It was bad enough that he sat just a few rows behind and she had to hear his voice. But what made things worse was that she could *feel* him.

Her nerves tingled, her hands shook and her heart pounded with awareness. She tried to talk to Savannah, but the woman was more interested in taking a nap before they arrived. Likewise, Mavoreen was snoring away in the row in front. Deanie was left with her magazines.

Unfortunately, makeup and clothes and *Fifty Ways to Make Your Man Say Wow* wasn't enough to distract her from the knowledge that he was there.

Behind her.

Watching her.

Even more, Rance himself reminded her every hour or so by heading to the men's restroom near the cockpit. On his way back to his seat, he made it a point to meet and hold her gaze. And he grinned at her. And forced her heartbeat faster with the twinkle in his eyes. She couldn't help but feel like the last barbecue rib at an Elks luncheon, and Rance was one hungry Elk.

Right.

No way did Rance actually hunger for her.

She told herself that as they flew the hundreds of miles to Miami, and she actually believed it by the time the plane touched down to pick up more passengers. But then they took off again and he made another bathroom trip, and the way he looked at her sparked the thought all over again.

Maybe he *was* telling the truth.

Maybe fate had orchestrated this chance meeting. Maybe they'd been thrown together so that their unspent lust for one another could be rekindled. At least her own would be rekindled. He hadn't carried a torch for her back then, so his lusty fire would have just ignited at the sight of her. Maybe he'd realized what he'd been missing all these years and he would do any and everything to make it up to her.

Forget Mavoreen. Deanie was the seriously delusional one.

He was following her, checking up on her, plain and simple. Reason told her as much.

If only Rance didn't keep stirring her doubt with his sexy-enough-to-be-a-sex-instructor grin.

Thankfully, the trip from Miami to Escapades Island was short. The Fasten Seat Belt light stayed on the entire time so Rance stayed in his seat. And Deanie managed to shake the whole attraction/fate theory.

"We have exactly twenty-two minutes before we take off for Eden," the flight attendant announced once they'd rolled to a stop at the main gate at the Escapades airport. "Until then, everyone is free to move around the cabin."

Uh, oh.

"This is where I get off," Savannah declared as she gathered her purse and pushed to her feet. "Nice meeting you and happy Valentine's Day."

"Thanks. You know," Deanie unfastened her seat belt and pushed to her feet, "I really need to stretch my legs. I'll walk you out." She followed Savannah down the aisle and up the terminal gate.

She wasn't going to be a sitting duck for Rance and her own crazy fantasies.

And if he follows you?

She didn't chance a glance over her shoulder. She wasn't risking even more eye contact if he *was* following her. She said goodbye to Savannah once they reached the gate and headed into the small but busy terminal that serviced all flights to and from Escapades Island. She passed a newsstand and a bagel cart before she felt the hair on the back of her neck prickle.

He was following her, all right, and she knew just how to prove it and kill the *maybe's* once and for all.

An instructor?

"My aunt Fanny," she muttered to herself as she picked up her steps and rounded a corner.

She pulled open a small door to her left and disappeared into the dark interior. Groping for the light switch, she held her hand in position and waited. A few seconds later, the doorknob trembled.

Metal hinges creaked and a shaft of light peaked into the dark interior. She inched to the left, deeper into the darkness and waited for the door to swing wider. The light grew brighter and a large, unmistakable form stepped inside.

3

"I KNEW IT!" She flipped on the switch and light flooded the small room. "You *are* following me."

"I am not." Rance frowned.

"Oh really? You're standing in an airport storage closet."

"So are you," he retorted. "Maybe you're the one following me."

"Excuse me? I was here first," she reminded him. "My brothers sent you here to spy on me, didn't they?"

His mouth thinned as if he were about to deny it. "Actually, they sent me to talk some sense into you," he finally said after a long moment.

She'd known the truth, but having it confirmed bothered her a lot more than she expected. Her chest tightened. She blinked against the sudden burning behind her eyes. "So all of that instructor stuff was just a bunch of BS?"

"They *are* always looking for qualified instructors according to their Web site."

"But you're not one of the chosen few."

"I could be. If I wanted to be."

"I should have known." *Hello? You did know.*

She just hadn't wanted to believe it. Deep down, she'd wanted to think that maybe Fate *had* finally smiled on her. Maybe all those years of dreaming hadn't been wasted. Maybe it had just been poor timing.

And now the time was right and he'd followed her because he'd wanted to.

Wrong.

"Look, I'm sorry I lied to you, but it was for a good cause. Clay is worried about you and I promised him I would stick close and keep an eye out. I was afraid you would have walked off the plane back in San Antonio if I didn't give you a convincing story."

"I would have."

"Which means it really was convincing."

"Then." She narrowed her gaze. "But now that I really think about it, I can see major holes."

His mouth tightened into a frown. "It's the tightest story I've ever heard."

"Not really. I know you have a reputation back

home, but it takes more than just a little backseat action to make a Camp E.D.E.N. instructor."

"A little?" He arched an eyebrow at her.

"Okay, so a lot. But that's small town stuff, which is always overexaggerated. Not to mention, that was years ago. You could have been celibate since then for all anyone knows. Which brings us to huge, gaping hole number one—you don't have any solid references behind you."

"I haven't been celibate."

"Says you."

"And the press," he reminded her.

"Everybody knows the media can blow things out of proportion. Last year Irma Sue Sinclair bought a push-up bra on a shopping trip to Austin. Two days later, the "About Town" column reported that she'd not only had her boobs done, but splurged on a tummy tuck and liposuction to boot."

"That's small-town gossip, not news."

"You're telling me that piece I saw on Inside Edition—the one with you eating a banana split off some centerfold's belly—was news?"

"It was for charity."

"It was for publicity. Look, I know you think you've maintained your reputation by ingesting all that whipped cream, but—"

"—and cherries."

"—and cherries," she added, ignoring the sudden vision that popped into her head of a very well-placed cherry and a certain tall, dark and handsome man trying to retrieve it with his mouth. "But just because you know your way around a seductive dessert, doesn't make you an expert when it comes to sex."

"Trust me." His gaze glittered gold fire and she became acutely aware of the small size of the closet and his close proximity. "I'm fully qualified in that department."

"That's what you say. But talking the talk doesn't make you a real expert. It takes moves. Skill. *Action.*" His frown deepened and she added, "If I were Camp E.D.E.N.'s owner, I would have only the most *experienced* instructors working for me. As a paying student, I expect a certain level of expertise."

"And you don't think I've reached that level?"

And then some. She shrugged. "It's nothing personal. Camp E.D.E.N. needs teachers who can put their money where their mouth is… What are you doing?" she blurted as he stepped closer and she lost the precious few inches of distance between them.

"Putting my money where my mouth is." He leaned down and his lips touched hers.

Deanie wasn't sure what she'd expected from Rance, but she was damned sure what she didn't expect.

A kiss.

A hot, wet, breath-stealing kiss.

Shock beat through her for the next few seconds as his lips nibbled at hers. But then he reached out, his large hands sliding around her waist, and her surprise faded amid the sudden tidal wave of lust that broke over her.

She slid her hands up and around his shoulders, his neck, and buried her fingers in his hair. His mouth slanted more fully over hers and his tongue plunged deep to tangle with hers. The kiss heated and shifted into overdrive as his hands slid down to cup her bottom and pull her tight against his hard crotch.

He rubbed her back and forth and she shuddered. He felt so good. So right.

Fate.

The word echoed in her head as she slid her hands beneath his T-shirt and stroked his bare skin. He reached between them and cupped her breast. He stroked the fullness through her thin sundress before sliding his fingers toward the gaping neckline. He traced the path where her plump skin plunged beneath the fabric and she trembled. His touch moved higher, following the strap that fastened around her neck. He paused over the hook and for a long moment, his hand cupped the back of her head and he simply kissed her. Deeply, thoroughly, his tongue stroking in a frenzied rhythm that picked her up like a tidal wave and carried her along for the ride.

She relished the taste and texture of him. A moan of protest curled up her throat when he finally pulled away. Her brain barely had time to register the fact that he'd unclasped the halter top of her dress and the material now bunched at her waist. Her bare breasts trembled from the sudden rush of air and she felt a moment of self-consciousness. But then he caught one nipple between his thumb and forefinger and squeezed, and a bolt of pleasure pierced her brain. Her lips parted on a gasp and then he was kissing her again.

Her hands dropped from his shoulders and traced a path down the hard wall of his chest. She pressed her palm over his erection, feeling him through the fabric of his shorts. She was this close to the zipper when the doorknob trembled.

Things happened fast in the next few seconds as Rance pulled away and caught the doorknob just as someone tried to open it from the other side.

"What the…" The voice carried from the other

side as Rance jerked the door shut and held it tight while Deanie fumbled to cover herself.

"Just a second," he called out, glancing at her to make sure she was fully covered. His eyes were a deep, dark gold. Surprise shimmered in their depths.

Surprise?

Because he'd kissed her, or because he'd liked it.

She didn't have time to debate the answer before she tightened the clasp on her dress and Rance loosened his grip on the doorknob. Metal creaked and the outside world intruded. Deanie's lust faded into a rush of anger as she stepped into the terminal and stared through the wall of windows that overlooked the boarding gate.

RANCE STOOD amid the hustle and bustle of the airport and let his gaze follow Deanie's. He stared at the empty spot where their plane had sat, the stairs now pulled back and idle, and frowned. At least, he tried to stare at the empty spot, but his gaze kept straying to the woman next to him.

He'd kissed Deanie Codge.

That fact didn't bother him half as much as the fact that he'd kissed her and he'd liked it.

Obviously, a lot more than she had.

"...can't be happening," she murmured, her

soft, panicked voice pushing past the whirlwind of his thoughts. "I have to check-in at Camp E.D.E.N. today or I'll lose my Valentine's Day discount."

"It's not Valentine's Day until tomorrow."

"That's beside the point. The course runs through Valentine's Day, and so they're giving a discount. It officially starts today." She glanced at her watch. "Check-in is less than an hour. And the first workshop is right after that."

"So you miss it. So what?"

"I can't just miss it. I paid for it. I *need* it…"

She was totally oblivious to him. To the fact that he'd kissed her senseless only minutes ago. To the fact that he was standing next to her and it was taking everything he had not to reach for her again.

He'd meant to teach her a lesson. To show her that he was every bit as good as his reputation maintained. Even more, to turn the tables and remind her that she wanted him.

She always had.

Then.

And now?

While she'd responded as if she still did, she'd managed to forget all about it in the face of their departed plane. As if she kissed and felt up men every day of the week. As if it hadn't been that big of a deal.

The notion stuck in Rance's craw as he followed her toward the desk at the boarding gate.

"We just missed our flight," Deanie told the attendant. "You have to call it back."

"I'm afraid we can't do that, miss. They've already taken off."

"Then put me on the next connecting flight," she said.

"Us," Rance cut in. "Put us on the next connecting flight."

"No problem." The woman tapped away at her computer keyboard for several seconds before a triumphant smile lit her face. "That will put you on Flight 1156 coming from Miami."

"When does it get here?"

"At three-fifteen."

"That's not so bad," Rance told her as he glanced at his watch. "You shouldn't miss more than one workshop. Two at the most."

"Three-fifteen tomorrow."

"But I need to be there today."

"I'm sorry, miss. There are no more flights today." She gave a brilliant smile. "But the airline will be happy to put you up at the island's main resort until your connecting flight arrives tomorrow. The resort is nearly full, but we reserve a few extra rooms for this sort of mishap. People miss flights all the time. Someone's always taking sick or getting stuck in the snack bar line. There was even this time when a woman actually fell asleep in the ladies' room—she suffered from that sleep disorder where you just conk out with no advance warning. Anyhow, we're fully prepared to deal with these situations."

"What about a boat? Can't I take a boat to the next island?"

"This is an airline, miss. Not a marina."

"But—" Deanie protested.

"Thanks," Rance cut in, taking the new flight itinerary that the attendant handed them. "We appreciate your help."

"Says you." Deanie turned on him, her gaze hard and glittering. He'd kissed away her pink lip gloss in the closet. Her lips were full and pouty. Or they would have been if she wasn't wearing such a tight frown. "This is all your fault."

He could argue that one. She'd turned him on with her sudden cold shoulder after all those years of panting after him, a calculated move to stir his interest if he'd ever seen one. On top of that, she'd insulted his *expertise,* no doubt knowing full well he'd be hard-pressed to prove her wrong.

Why, she'd practically begged for that kiss.

That's what he told himself. He just wasn't so

sure he believed it, especially since she was currently staring daggers at him.

"Let's go." He took the complimentary room passes the attendant handed him and steered her around. He did his damnedest to ignore the warm pull of heat at his fingertips as he steered her through the small airport as fast as he could manage without running someone down.

He needed out of there. He needed some fresh air. He needed a cold shower.

What he didn't need was another trip to the storage closet.

But man-o-man, did he want one.

RANCE WATCHED DEANIE walk toward the cab that waited at the curb. Sunlight drenched her, outlining her petite figure clad in the hot pink sundress.

An honest-to-god *figure,* with enough curves and indentations to make his mouth water.

Not that he'd ever doubted she actually had one. He'd just never really thought about it until that night at the creek.

Up until then, she'd been Teeny Deanie. His buddy's kid sister. His personal pain-in-the-ass.

Speaking of asses…

His gaze hooked on the gentle sway of her tight, round bottom beneath the short pink dress and his stomach hollowed out. For a split second, he imagined bending her over, peeling the dress up and sinking his fingers into her soft pale flesh. He imagined sinking something else into her, as well, and his groin throbbed its agreement. He licked his lips and tasted sweet, sugary candy and something else. Something rich and potent that made his gut ache for another taste.

"I have no intention of tagging along after you."

Her words echoed in his head as he watched her fold herself into the cab and pull the door shut behind her, and he frowned. She was telling the truth. While he'd tried to convince himself that her indifference had just been an act to stir his interest, he knew better.

While she was still attracted to him—there was no mistaking her response to his kiss—she didn't *want* to be attracted to him.

She wanted to start a new life.

To put the past behind her.

To forget him and, from the way she motioned for the cab driver to take off, make him walk from the small airport to the resort.

He picked up his steps as bitterness swirled inside him and made his throat tight.

Forget him?

After all they'd shared, she wanted to chuck it

all and wipe the slate clean. Hell, she didn't even seem to give a lick that he'd broken his leg not four months ago and was, most likely, in some serious pain with all this walking.

Okay, so they hadn't actually *shared* anything, except a few cookies, the occasional slice of cake and the every-now-and-then bag of his favorite jawbreakers. But that had been his fault. He'd resisted her advances and done his best to discourage her, at least romantically. He'd had nothing against talking to her when she sat next to him on the bus or showed up on his doorstep.

Christ, he'd *liked* talking to her.

There'd been no need to search for the right words to try to impress her. She'd liked him anyway. Even more, she'd listened and understood everything he'd had to say.

And even the stuff he hadn't been able to say.

He could still remember the time he'd been shooting marbles with a group of boys in the schoolyard. She'd been in the first grade and he'd been in the fifth, and she'd just started following him around. He'd had the biggest collection of marbles out of all the boys, and he'd been dead certain he was good enough to keep them.

He'd been wrong.

There had been a new kid at school and he'd been

better. Rance had lost all of his marbles that day, and most of the ones that belonged to his two brothers.

Rance remembered crying only two times in his life. That had been the first time. He'd gone home and bawled his eyes out. He'd been bawling, as a matter of fact, when Deanie had come knocking. She'd held a great big bag of jawbreakers in her small hands.

"Jawbreakers?" He swiped at his tears and sniffled.

"For the ones you lost," she told him.

"They weren't jawbreakers, doofus. They were marbles. I can't shoot jawbreakers."

She frowned as she stared at the bag, as if thinking hard for the first time. And then she smiled and popped one into her mouth. "No, but you can eat them."

She held the bag out to him and he had the urge to tell her to get lost. But something about the way she looked at him, her blue eyes warm and full of understanding, made him want to reach out.

He took a jawbreaker and popped it into his mouth. Cherry exploded on his tongue and he smiled, too.

She'd been there the second time in his life when he'd cried, as well. He'd been sixteen then and he'd just lost both his parents. He'd barely arrived home after the double funeral before the townsfolk had started to arrive. They'd brought everything from ham to casseroles. Miss Jackie had brought her famous red velvet cake and Miss Myrtle had brought homemade bread and strawberry preserves. But he hadn't had an appetite for any of it. He'd felt sick inside. Empty. Dead.

And then he'd opened the door to find Deanie standing there with a great big bag of jawbreakers. She hadn't said a word. No "I'm sorry for your loss" or "Let me know if I can do anything." She'd just stared at him with her bright blue eyes and popped a candy into her mouth. Then she'd handed the bag to him.

He'd done the same and while he'd sucked the cherry coating off, he'd actually felt better.

As the memories swirled in his head, he couldn't help the sudden feeling that maybe he'd been a genuine dumb ass back then. Maybe Deanie had been the perfect girl and he just hadn't been able to see past her T-shirts, baggy jeans or mud-covered cowboy boots.

Maybe he shouldn't have walked away that night down by the creek.

And maybe your pride's just hurt, buddy.

Maybe. Probably.

There was only one way to prove it.

If the lust eating him up from the inside out was the result of his wounded ego, it would fade once he and Deanie had a good, old-fashioned roll in the hay. Then she could get on with her "education" and he could stop thinking those damnable what-ifs.

And if it didn't?

As soon as the question struck, Rance squashed it. It would. He had his flaws, but he couldn't have been *that* blind. Any more than he could have said yes to her that night. She'd been too young and he'd been too old, and it just wouldn't have been right.

He picked up his steps, careful to add a nice, pained looking limp to his gait, and called out. "Wait up!"

She turned toward him and he caught her stare.

Suspicion glimmered in her true blue gaze, but not before he'd seen the flash of concern. She said something to the driver, leaned over and shoved open the door.

Rance grinned and climbed in next to her.

4

DEANIE WANTED to strangle him.

The moment they were out of the cab, and out of sight of any witnesses, she intended to slide her hands around his strong, taut, tanned throat and squeeze. Her fingers flexed from the memory of his warm skin beneath her fingertips and anticipation zipped along her nerve endings.

Forget strangling. She needed a noncontact, long-distance way to do him in. Guilt snuck through her for a split second. After all, this was Rance. Her one and only. *The* man.

Then, she reminded herself.

So what if he'd shared his lunch with her the time she'd forgotten hers? Or that he'd been the first boy—nonrelative, that is—she'd ever danced with? Or that he'd always jumped in when anyone bigger had been picking on her? Heck, he'd even jumped in when one of her own brothers had given her a hard time.

Not that she'd needed his interference. She'd had a right hook her brothers had feared.

But it *had* felt good when he'd taken up for her.

She slid a sideways glance at him and his stare caught hers. His lips tilted in a knowing grin and a rush of heat bolted through her. Only a few feet of vinyl separated them in the small cab. She could feel the heat from his body. Smell the delicious aroma of fresh air, clean soap and confidence that was all Rance McGraw.

He was confident, all right. He'd intentionally screwed up her plans.

For now. But in twenty-four hours, she was climbing back onto that plane and continuing with her trip. Regardless of what he had up his sleeve.

Or in his pants.

She remembered the feel of his groin pressed into her stomach and her nipples pebbled.

Bad nipples.

She inched closer to the door, rolled down the window and let the island breeze cool her hot cheeks. Her mind rewinded back to her earlier train of thought. Murder. Noncontact.

Maybe a gun. Or even a rock. She *had* had a pretty good aim with a slingshot way back when. Her oldest brother, Cory, still had a scar where she'd nailed him when he'd been taunting her from his tree house. He'd been twelve and she'd been five—too young to actually climb up—and so she'd fired away. He'd squawked and hit the ground like a sack of potatoes.

She smiled at the memory.

"What are you thinking?" Rance asked.

"Of effective ways to eliminate you."

"I'm serious."

"So am I." She leveled a stare at him and focused on the aggravation bubbling inside her. "I don't like being manipulated."

"It was a kiss, Teeny."

"To manipulate me into changing my mind about this trip, which I'm not going to do. You can just call Clay, tell him I'm a big girl and that I don't need a babysitter."

Silence settled between them for several long moments as they sped down the palm tree-lined road that led to the island's one and only resort. She fixed her gaze on the passing landscape and tried to tune out his presence.

"You really are mad, aren't you?" he finally asked.

"Yes."

"Hey," he grinned and leaned toward her as if he'd just thought of some great secret that would make everything better. "You remember that time Bobby McFarland climbed onto the bus with that hunk of dry ice in his lunch kit? He dumped his soda on it and it started smoking, and the bus driver thought he'd started a fire. So we were stranded."

A smile tugged at her lips. It *had* been sort of funny.

They'd all sat on the side of the road until Romeo's one and only fire truck had rolled up to examine the situation—the driver had been freaked out and had ordered everyone to evacuate the bus. She'd refused to walk back on and assess the "fire" herself. They'd been three hours late to school that day.

One of the best days of Deanie's life.

Not only had she missed her fourth grade spelling test she hadn't had time to study for, but she'd spent the extra time playing tic-tac-toe with Rance. And talking. And laughing.

Since none of her brothers had been on the bus with her that morning—two had been home with the flu and the other three had had to go in early to work on various projects—Deanie had had Rance's complete attention. While there had been a dozen other kids to choose from, he'd sat with her.

He'd liked her.

But he hadn't *liked* her. She hadn't been pretty

enough or girlie enough to stir anything more than friendship, and so he'd never so much as kissed her.

Until now.

Her gaze fell to her lap where she'd placed her hands. They looked pale against the hot pink material. She tried to wiggle her toes, but the high heels hugged her feet too tight. She drew in a deep breath and felt her breasts press against the snug bodice.

She certainly looked different now, but she wasn't foolish enough to think it had sparked his sudden interest.

"At least we're stranded smack dab in the middle of paradise this time," his deep voice drew her from her thoughts before she could think too hard about the question.

"The Travel Channel's Number One Caribbean Hot Spot," the driver chimed in from the front seat.

"That's right," Rance added. "Number one spot."

"Whatever you like—scuba, snorkeling, fishing, waterskiing—the hotel can hook you up," the driver added. "And don't forget to try The Falls."

"What's that?" Rance asked.

"A five star restaurant built around a natural waterfall fed lagoon. They've got the best stuffed crabs around and they make a great pineapple margarita."

"You could definitely use one of those," Rance told Deanie. "You're much too uptight."

"I'm not uptight. I'm angry," she reminded him. "In case you've forgotten, I'm supposed to be somewhere else right now. Doing something else. With someone else."

His grin disappeared and he drew his lips tight. "Sex."

"Sex education," she corrected, doing her best to ignore the flutter in her stomach when she saw the jealous light in his gaze.

Jealous? If only, a voice whispered.

She ignored a sudden burst of longing. "Camp E.D.E.N. is going to help me get in touch with my inner vixen. I need to unlock my sexuality to fully enjoy and experience it, and they're going to give me the key—" Her words drowned in the shrill ring of a cell phone.

Rance held up a hand for her to hold on and pulled the slim silver contraption from his pocket. He punched the on button. "Yeah? No, don't make the arrangements from San Antonio. I'll be flying out from the Caribbean." He grew silent for a few seconds as he listened. "I don't know right now. I'll let you know. Look, Shank, you've got to calm down about this stuff before you give yourself a heart attack." Silence. "I've got something to take care of first, but I'll be there. Have I ever let you down?" Obviously, the answer was no because the conversation ended without any more explanation.

"Sorry," he told her after he'd punched the off button and slid the cell back into his pocket. "My business partner is getting a little antsy." At her arched eyebrow, he added, "I'm due in Australia for a competition this weekend." He wiped a hand over his face. "I'm supposed to fly out tomorrow for some preliminary media events."

"So you figured in the meantime, you would talk some sense into me, change my mind, put me on a plane back home and then you could fly out tomorrow as planned?"

He looked as if he wanted to deny it, but then he shrugged. "That would have been the best-case scenario."

"The worst case being that you would have to miss your competition and babysit me the entire two weeks?"

"Actually, I was thinking worst case, as in I hog-tie you, tape your mouth shut, and put you on the first plane back home."

"While you fly off to wrestle porcupines in the Amazon."

"I wrangled snakes in the Amazon. This is an alligator wrestling competition. *The* alligator wrestling competition of the year. Competitors come from all over the world."

"Sounds exciting."

"It is," he said, but the certainty didn't touch his eyes. Deanie knew then that while Rance was living the extreme dream, he hadn't found any extreme happiness to go along with it.

"Is it harder than steer wrestling?"

"No. You just get a lot wetter."

"Is it as much fun?"

No. The answer was there in his eyes, but it didn't make it past his lips. "Stop trying to change the subject."

"You brought it up," she told him. "What can I say?" She shrugged. "I'm curious."

"Not half as curious as you are stubborn. Christ, Deanie," he murmured, his voice suddenly softer. "A *sex* camp?"

"I know how it sounds, but it's run like any other school."

"You don't learn how to have great sex by sitting in a classroom, listening to a lecture. Have you ever just thought about kicking back and letting your natural impulses take over?"

"The only place I've ever gotten by 'kicking back' is last place."

She had *last* written all over her. Back in kindergarten when she'd been too small to reach the water fountain like the other kids. In junior high when the tallest girl in the class had stolen Deanie's science homework and hidden it at the top of the locker which had been out of arm's reach.

She swallowed against the sudden lump in her throat and fought the urge to slide across the seat and press her body into his embrace.

Because when he'd held her, *kissed* her in that storage room, she hadn't thought about the past or the future or the fact that she was still a far cry from the confident, experienced, ultra-femme female she wanted to be. She hadn't thought, period.

She'd simply *felt,* and it had felt really right.

"Things don't just fall into place for me," she said, eager for a distraction from the truth—that she still had it bad for Rance McGraw. "Some of us are born lucky and some have to make our own luck. Unfortunately, I'm in group two."

"And which one am I in?"

"Let's see… You're not bad on the eyes." Talk about the understatement of the century. "You were junior steer wrestling champion four years in a row. Captain of the football team, both high school and then college. All state. First draft pick. Two Super Bowl rings. A successful business."

"I busted my ass for all of that." She gave him

a pointed look and he shrugged. "All of it except the *not bad on the eyes.*"

"Then you know what I'm talking about."

"I'm not saying you shouldn't have a plan or set your mind to it. But sex is different. It's all about finding your groove."

"What if you don't have a groove?" she asked before she could stop herself. "I mean, not that I don't," she rushed on, eager to hide her sudden insecurity. It was one thing for him to deduce that her registration at Camp E.D.E.N. meant she was totally inept in bed, and quite another for her to confirm it out loud. "I just want to perfect mine."

"Then all you need is a little practice." *With me,* his gaze seemed to say.

Yeah, right. Rance McGraw interested in Deanie Codge? That was a laugh.

Then again, she wasn't the same old Deanie.

She was the new and improved version with her hot pink dress and leg-enhancing high heels and newfound cleavage. Maybe he really did see her differently now.

The thought should have sent a wave of satisfaction rippling through her. Instead, she frowned.

"What I need is a boat," she muttered. Surely they had charters traveling to the various islands?

"Why don't you just stop all this nonsense,

forget about Camp E.D.E.N. and enjoy the next twenty-four hours?" he asked as they pulled to a stop in front of the hotel.

Fat chance, with Rance McGraw dogging her every footstep. With him so close, it was too easy to forget everything except their kiss and how much she wanted another one and how she would do practically anything if he would just… *No*.

She wasn't going there. Not this time.

Not ever again.

"I CAN'T BELIEVE you sicced Rance McGraw on me," Deanie said into the phone the moment her brother Clay's answering machine beeped. She hesitated a moment, wondering if Helen had gone into labor, which would explain why her brother hadn't picked up the phone himself. If something had happened to her sister-in-law, Clay would have called. Deanie had already listened to all of her messages, and there wasn't one mention of Helen or the baby. He was probably out riding fence while their father played bingo at the diner and Helen shopped for another baby outfit.

"First off, my business is none of your business," she told his machine after she'd reassured herself. "And second, my business is none of Rance's business. And third, I can't wait until

I get back because I'm going to really enjoy telling Helen *your* business. Particularly about your so-called business trip to Sioux City. The one where you went fishing when you should have been home with her helping her pick out flowers for the wedding. Why, I bet she'll have no problem understanding how you'd rather gut a trout than pick out the perfect breed of rose for your fiancée's bouquet." *Click*.

Okay, so she had no intention of telling Helen and hurting her feelings, but it would serve Clay right if she did. Even more, she didn't want to be the only person losing a night of sleep. He deserved to toss and turn a little.

Her gaze slid to Rance who sprawled in a lobby chair, his hat tipped back, his gaze as handsome as ever as he studied his surroundings.

He should have been in the elevator, headed for the eighteenth floor and his hotel room. *Their* hotel room. They'd presented their comp tickets to the woman at the registration desk only to find that Escapades had only double rooms available—they were primarily a couples paradise, after all. Which meant that Deanie and Rance could share a complimentary double, or pay the outrageous price for an additional double.

While Deanie had no doubt that Rance could

afford it, he'd merely drawled in that slow, deep voice of his, "One double will be just fine with me," and taken the key card the woman had handed over. Meanwhile, Deanie hadn't been about to blow an obscene amount of money on a room without first weighing all of her options. After all, Camp E.D.E.N. wasn't all that far away. If she hurried, she could still make the first scheduled workshop.

Rance's gaze collided with hers and he grinned. He was waiting for her.

Watching her.

Wanting her.

Her stomach flipped and she had a sudden vision of a moonlit hotel room. The white sheers ruffled with the island breeze as it blew through the open patio doors. Rance's tall, tanned body sprawled across the white sheets of a king-size bed…

Her heart skipped a beat and she drew a deep, calming breath.

Okay, so Clay deserved to toss and turn a heck of a lot for this one. In fact, we're talking major insomnia. With a few paranoid delusions thrown in.

She forced her gaze from Rance to the display of brochures just to her left. Her attention fixed on Madame Zombobwee's House of Voodoo.

She reached for the colorful advertisement.

Maybe she would pay the woman a visit this afternoon if she didn't manage to get off Escapades and over to Camp E.D.E.N. A voodoo doll and a few well-placed pins and Clay would surely regret butting into her life.

Folding the brochure, she stuffed it into her purse and headed for the concierge desk. "I need a boat," she told the young man wearing a starched white and blue floral shirt, creased khaki slacks and a nametag that read Alan At Your Service.

"I'm afraid all of the fishing charters left early this morning."

"I don't want to fish. I want a ride to a neighboring island. Camp E.D.E.N."

"There's a sightseeing tour that travels around the nearby islands, but I'm afraid that left early, as well. It's an all day even with lunch *and* dinner. Not that they stop off at Eden. That's a privately owned island."

"I know. I've booked a course there. Orientation is this afternoon." His gaze widened and a twinkle lit his eyes. "Aren't there any private boats?" she asked before he could make some sort of cheesy comment. "For emergencies?"

His knowing gaze disappeared and concern drew his eyebrows tight. "What's your emergency?"

I need to learn how to Shed My Inhibitions.

"Never mind." She glanced at the various pamphlets sitting on the desk. Her gaze zeroed in on one and an idea struck. "What about a Wave Runner?"

He smiled. "We have plenty of those. We rent them by the hour. Unfortunately, the hotel is full and demand is high, so they're booked up a full day in advance. But you can add your name to the waiting list in case someone doesn't show. Just see the reservations desk out by the North Pool." He pointed to the rear of the lobby and a pair of glass doors.

Beyond, the white sand beach shimmered in the midday sunlight. Palm trees swayed with a faint breeze. Blue water stretched endlessly, the horizon dotted only by the distant spot that represented Camp E.D.E.N.

She was *this* close.

All she needed was a way to get there.

She gathered up her purse, ignored the urge to glance in Rance's direction one last time, and headed through the lobby toward the rear of the hotel.

She thought for all of five minutes that Rance had given up following her. The sofa where he'd been sitting now held an elderly couple who sat side-by-side and held each other's hand, their gazes full of adoration as they stared at one another.

A pang of longing shot through her. While she

was fixated on self-improvement at the moment, it was really just the means to an end. She wanted her own happily ever after. She wanted to fall in love. Even more, she wanted to fall in love with a man who would love her back. Unfortunately Rance wasn't even a contender.

Even so, she found herself looking for him as she left the lobby and made her way around the monstrous pool.

An up-beat salsa tune blared from the patio speakers. The pool practically overflowed with oil-slicked bodies. Waiters rushed here and there with trays of drinks. A string of paper hearts had been taped across the bar in honor of the following Saturday. A huge red and white balloon arch framed the far side of the pool where a band was scheduled to play a special Valentine's dinner and dance the following day.

Her thoughts rushed back to a certain Valentine's Day when she'd been ten and still desperately, openly infatuated with the best looking boy in town.

She'd spent an entire morning baking cookies, and fighting with her brothers who'd been scarfing them down as fast as she could pull them from the oven. She'd managed to salvage a baker's dozen from the seventy-eight she'd made and pack them into a shoe box lined with wax paper. She'd waited until Rance had stepped off the school bus and then presented him with her box of goodies.

The next year she'd given him a homemade red velvet cake.

The year after that, heart-shaped cupcakes.

The year after that, the largest box of chocolates from the general store.

She'd been persistent, and he'd been nice, but it hadn't made him see her as anything other than a friend.

He'd graduated and gone off to college and she hadn't celebrated the holiday since. Sure, she'd had several boyfriends over the years, but she'd never actually been in a relationship when the fourteenth rolled around, and so she'd never had a *real* Valentine's Day.

Deanie shook off the sudden depressing thought and stepped toward the grass hut that served as the registration desk.

She smiled at the young man who stood behind the counter. He was tall, tanned and blonde and wore the familiar blue floral print shirt and starched khakis. His name tag read Malcolm At Your Service.

"Malcolm, I need to rent a Wave Runner."

The hair on the back of her neck prickled and she felt Rance's presence even before she heard his voice.

"Make that two." He came up behind her, so close that she felt the heat from his hard body.

"Sure," the attendant said as he retrieved his clipboard. "I should have a pair available..." He studied the schedule on the clipboard. "Tomorrow evening," he finally announced. He smiled. "Name?"

"I really need one sooner than that. Can you put me on the list if someone cancels?"

"Yes ma'am, but I seriously doubt we'll have two cancellations at the same time. The Wave Runners are our most popular water sport right now since two of our dive boats are out of commission."

"That's okay," Deanie told the young man. "We're not together. He's headed for some porcupine-wrestling competition tomorrow and I'm on my way to Camp E.D.E.N." She gave the young man her name and tried to ignore the annoyed look on Rance's face as she turned to head back into the lobby to fork over the money for her own room. She could have sworn she even heard him growl as she breezed by without so much as a "see you later."

As if he wanted them to be *together.*

He didn't.

He was here on behalf of her brother. He'd kissed her on behalf of her brother—to make her miss her plane and stop her from reaching Eden.

He was stalking her—for the next twenty-four hours—on behalf of her brother.

He wasn't acting of his own free will.

Thankfully.

Because if he had been the slightest bit sincere, Deanie would have been hard-pressed to remember the promise she'd made to herself that night at the river—namely that she would never, ever offer herself again to Rance McGraw.

No matter how much she wanted to jump his delectable body right now.

5

"Too old." The deep, familiar drawl slid into Deanie's ears and her hand paused just shy of the panties hanging on the small lingerie rack in the hotel's one and only clothing shop.

After registering for her own hotel room, she'd gone inside to pick up some things to see her through until tomorrow since she was obviously stuck for the next twenty-four hours. That, and she'd been desperate to steer clear of Rance.

It seemed, however, that he wasn't like her older brothers who would rather cut off an arm than go shopping.

She felt the heat of his body at her back. His scent—prime male and fresh soap and danger with a capital D—filled her head. Her heart stalled and her tummy tingled.

"Excuse me?" she managed to say.

"If you're serious about this whole inner vixen thing, I can tell you she wouldn't want you to wear those." He indicated the white cotton briefs she'd been about to pick up. "Why don't you try that little black number right there."

"I can't wear black underwear with this." She held up the pale floral print sundress she'd just picked out.

"You're right. You should just go natural."

The comment stirred a fantasy of Rance sitting next to her on the plane as they both headed for Camp E.D.E.N., his hand on her knee, sliding beneath the hem of the new sundress, up the inside of her thigh to the very naked heart of her...

Heat zigzagged through her body. Her nipples tingled and her thighs clenched. She stiffened.

Reality check. She wasn't supposed to react to him. She'd promised herself *not* to react to him. Her days of lusting after Rance McGraw were completely over.

O-V-E-R.

Even if she had fallen from grace in the airport storage closet. That had been a cold, calculated move on his part to mess up her plans. Besides, she hadn't initiated the kiss. He had.

Which meant she hadn't broken her promise to herself.

She frowned at him. "Don't you have some shopping of your own to do?" Without waiting for a reply, she turned and moved a few steps away toward a stack of T-shirts.

"I though I'd help you out." He shook his head at a T-shirt she picked up and reached for a skimpy tank top. "If you want sexy, this is the way to go."

"Thanks, but no thanks. I can manage fine on my own." She ignored the tank top and busied herself reaching for a cap-sleeved white tee, the words Island Princess spelled out in pink rhinestones.

"Maybe so, but I figure I owe you. You're missing today's workshops because of me."

"Which was your goal in the first place. So why the sudden touch of guilt?"

"I said I would keep an eye on you and keep you out of trouble. I didn't say I would stop you."

"So you didn't purposely try to make me miss my flight?"

"Trust me. That wasn't what I was thinking when I kissed you."

"It was just a convenient by-product." When he didn't deny the statement, she added, "So helping me pick out clothes will ease your conscience?"

"No. Giving you sex lessons will do that." When she simply stared at him, he added, "Just because you're missing the first day doesn't mean you have to miss today's workshops." His gaze caught and held hers. "I can teach you everything you need to know."

I'm not interested. Not anymore. Not ever again. That's what she wanted to say. But the words couldn't seem to make it past her heart which had jumped into her throat at the prospect of being Rance's *student*.

Not that she was about to say "yes" either.

She wanted a real education with reliable, step-by-step instruction in everything from Shedding Your Inhibitions and The Power Of Touching to Getting Into The E-Zone and Using Your Environment. While she had to give Rance his due—he was hot, hunky and undoubtedly experienced—he wasn't a professional like Drill Sergeant Meryl and his Ph.D. wife, Dr. Linda.

With Rance, there would be no no-nonsense lectures or educational films. No actual textbook. No class notes.

Just Rance smiling down at her, his large, tanned hand covering hers, guiding her over her own body in hit and miss until they'd discovered every vital pleasure point…

Okay, so he *had* screwed up her plans. Royally.

She was starting a brand-new job in two weeks, which meant she wouldn't be getting any time off for at least a year. Forget registering for Camp

E.D.E.N.'s next session and making up the workshops she'd missed. The only time she had to get in touch with her sexuality was right now. Right here.

With him.

But it was more than timing that chipped away at her resolve and urged her to say yes. As much as Deanie wanted to deny her attraction to him, she couldn't. Even after all these years, she still wanted him. More so now because she was all grown up. Forget daydreaming about his kisses. She wanted to feel him over her, inside of her, surrounding her.

This was it. Her chance. A once in a lifetime chance. Her dream come true. The dream she'd denied herself since that painful moment when she'd offered herself to him and he'd turned her down.

Never again, she'd promised herself.

But she wasn't the one offering. He was.

It was Rance who waited for her answer. Rance who wondered what she was thinking. Rance who risked his pride should she give in to the need for vengeance that burned deep inside her and refuse him.

But greater than the need for revenge was her need for him. To touch him. To taste him. To feel him.

She had twenty-four hours before they went

their separate ways again. Only this time, Deanie wouldn't be left with fantasies to warm her nights. She would have bona fide memories.

And some much-needed knowledge when it came to sex.

"I guess it really *is* the least you can do," she told him. If she hadn't known better, she would have sworn she saw relief flash in his gaze.

But then he smiled, his eyes twinkled, and he was the old Rance again. Full of self-confidence and sex appeal, and not the least bit worried about either.

"So how do we do this?" she asked him.

"That's what I'm going to teach you, Teeny." He gave her a quick kiss on the lips and winked. "Meet me at the main pool in a half hour."

"The pool? But wouldn't your hotel room be more appropriate…" Her words faded as he disappeared into the main lobby.

O-kay.

Maybe he wanted to go for a swim first. Get his heart pumping before he did the actual deed. One of her old boyfriends, Earl Connally, had liked to watch NASCAR before they got up close and personal because he said it really got his adrenaline pumping.

Deanie couldn't really picture Rance glued to

a television set, a beer in one hand and a Jimmie Johnson pennant in the other, but what did she know about men?

Very little.

She had exactly four ex-boyfriends. Earl the lube guy from the local Oil Express. Darnell who'd worked at the auto parts store. Bart the physical education teacher at Romeo Junior High. And Harwin the brake specialist at Big Daddy's. They'd all been nice guys—except for Harwin— who hadn't been any more experienced when it came to sex than Deanie herself.

And so all of her past encounters hadn't been anywhere close to the hot, spicy stuff of an erotica novel. In fact, she would have to qualify them as more fitting for an inspirational—Deanie had spent most of her time praying for things to hurry up and be over.

The old Deanie, that is.

She was the new and improved version now. A sexually confident, experienced, one hundred percent bona fide woman.

Or she soon would be once she started her training and reached out to her inner vixen.

She spent the next ten minutes choosing a swimsuit and wrap to go with her sundress. And new sandals that were featured in the front display case. They were a pair of barely-there two-inch heels with tiny bronze straps that crisscrossed at the toes and wrapped around the ankles.

Her toes curled at the prospect. The old Deanie wouldn't be caught dead in anything but her work boots or a pair of sneakers. Then again, the old Deanie wouldn't have purchased a leopard print bikini—also from the display case—that begged for man-killer shoes.

The whole get-up screamed *Sports Illustrated Swimsuit Edition* and was just the sort of thing somebody like Savannah Sierra Ellington would wear.

Deanie gathered her purchases and headed for the cash register. As she passed a ring of T-shirts and sweat pants, insecurity welled inside her and she found herself reaching out. It wasn't like she was going to wear the dreaded things. Not out in public. But if she wanted to relax in her room, there was certainly nothing wrong with being comfortable.

She grabbed her size and kept walking. When she reached the lingerie rack, she paused for an indecisive moment before adding the skimpy black thong to her pile.

Hey, Rance *was* the teacher.

For the next twenty-four hours, that is.

"SO HOW DO WE DO THIS?"

Deanie's soft, sweet voice echoed through Rance's head and followed him out into the lobby.

His heart pounded and his muscles bunched and his breaths came quicker. For a man who'd just made a touchdown and nailed the first quarter, he didn't feel nearly the relief or satisfaction he'd expected. Instead, he felt wired, nervous, *anxious*. For more.

For her.

At the same time, he couldn't shake the niggle of guilt that sat in his gut. After all, he'd just offered sex lessons to his best friend's baby sister. Clay would surely go ballistic.

At the same time, the baby sister had turned into one hell of a woman. A woman determined to beef up her sexual arsenal, with or without his help.

Rance frowned and his determination grew. If Deanie was dead set on getting an education in sex, he intended to be the one to give it to her. Better him than some stranger. Even Clay would understand that.

At least Rance hoped he would.

"Hey, Mr. McGraw! Wait up!"

Rance turned at the sound of the familiar voice.

Erica hurried after him. She wore the standard hotel staff fare with her black slacks and crisp white blouse. Only the three extra studs in her right ear hinted that she might be more daredevil than manager-in-training.

"I called my folks just after you checked in and my dad all but flipped when I told him that you were here. He followed you back when you were playing pro ball with the Cowboys. He never missed a game."

"Tell him I appreciate that."

"Actually, I was hoping you could tell him." She gave him a pleading look. "I was wondering if you wouldn't mind giving me an autograph." She pulled out an Extreme Dream T-shirt and a black Sharpie, and handed him both.

"You have a lot of these lying around?" he asked as she motioned him over to a nearby sitting area.

"Are you kidding?" She sat down and reached for one of the travel magazines scattered across the glass coffee table. "They're the total shit with everybody who's anybody. Surfers, wakers, skiers—you name it. I ordered this one online for my dad's birthday— he's always been a big fan. The autograph will make it that much more special." She handed the magazine to Rance who sank down into a nearby chair.

He grinned and slipped the booklet inside of the

shirt. "What's your dad's name?" He balanced the shirt on his lap and pulled the cap off the pen.

"Ralph."

Rance grinned, wrote a few sentences and signed his name. "Here you go."

"Thanks so much." She took the T-shirt, pulled out the magazine and replaced it on the coffee table. Her gaze drank in the sentiment he'd written. "He's going to totally love this."

"Glad I could help." Rance pushed to his feet and Erica followed. "I really need to run. I'm meeting someone."

"Sure. Listen, if you get bored while you're here, my friends and I meet at sunup every morning down at the marina for a little water sports jam to get the day started right. You're welcome to join us. We wakeboard, ski, windsurf. Just pick your poison."

"Thanks." He handed her back the Sharpie. "I'll keep that in mind."

"And remember, if you need anything while you're here, just let me know."

Rance's gaze caught Deanie as she exited the boutique and headed for the elevator.

The workshops from the Camp E.D.E.N. course curriculum played through his head and stirred several interesting visuals.

If he was going to seduce Deanie past the point of no return so that she would willingly, desperately offer herself up to him the way she had that night down by the creek, he was going to need some help. He needed every seductive tool he could find.

"Actually, there are a couple of things…"

YOU CAN DO THIS.

The affirmation played in Deanie's head as she stepped out of her hotel room and walked the few steps to the elevator.

Women did it all the time.

Tall, leggy, do-me women, a small voice whispered as the elevator doors slid open.

All types of women, the more courageous side of her chimed in. She eased her way between several people, glanced to make sure the lobby button was lit, and leaned against the far wall as the doors closed. Her stomach hollowed as the elevator dropped and she swallowed.

Why, even Pastor Cushing's wife did it on Sunday mornings, and Sister Maybelle was about as tall and leggy as a rhino. As for the *do-me* part…

Deanie shook away the thought.

She was *not* going there.

The bottom line—women of all ages, from all

walks of life, owned high heels and managed to wear them without eating pavement.

Which meant Deanie could do the same.

"Feet don't fail me now," she murmured several seconds later as she reached the ground floor. She stepped off the elevator, carefully rounded the corner and started across the marble-tiled floor.

She wore her new swimsuit and a matching cover up that wrapped around her like a sarong. She carried her new oversized straw bag stuffed full of essentials—sunscreen, her wallet, her hotel key card, sunscreen, her baseball cap, her cell phone—turned off, of course, to avoid Clay—sunscreen, a water bottle, a sports drink and sunscreen.

While Deanie had lived half her life outdoors, she'd learned early on to always be careful. Her dad had watched his own father die with skin cancer and so he'd been a fanatic about his kids protecting themselves while out and about.

And then there was Miss Janie from Senior Women's Rotary Club. Deanie had been giving Miss Janie's old Pontiac oil changes for the past five years since her husband had passed away, and so she knew all about Miss Janie's cousin's sister's husband who'd died of skin cancer just this last year.

Deanie thought of the old woman and she

couldn't help herself. She sat down in a nearby chair and rummaged for her cell phone. She had one message from Clay, no doubt denying he'd sent Rance after her, and two from Miss Margie.

She saved Clay's for later and listened as the message beeped. The old woman's voice came over the line.

"Deanie? Honey, if you're there pick up the phone."

Miss Margie had yet to grasp the concept of a cell phone message and always assumed she was talking to a traditional answering machine.

"Honey, I know you're making a change and all, but I really wish that change involved my oil. Why, that good-fer-nothing Harwin couldn't change oil if his life depended on it. Do you know he tried to put that cheap stuff in my engine? I told him you always put the quarter weight and charge me for the cheap stuff, but he refused to do it. Said it was dishonest and I told him that it was dishonest to be picking quarters out of the collection plate at church. He swore it wasn't him, but Genevive MacIntosh saw him with her good eye just last Sunday." Genevive had lost one eye to glaucoma and could only see with her left. "Lordy, I don't know what we're going to do around here without you. I'll have to dip into the nest egg that Norman

left me just to keep the car running smoothly
'cause now it's making this knocking sound something awful. I thought it was my hearing aid at first
on account of it's been acting funny since I got that
microwave oven. I knew that fancy thing would
mess up everything. It's as bad as one of them
tanning beds. Why, Jenny Lou's daughter just
happened to be wearing one of those TENS unit
stimulators on account of her back got messed up
from working in her garden when she went to pick
up her daughter at that new tanning salon Fake-n-
Bake over on Main Street. Anyhow, she didn't
even go past the front door and the darned TENS
unit went crazy. Starting ringing and vibrating.
Her doctor said it could have been the ultraviolet
rays, which I know it was. What do you know, but
I read in my microwave manual that it gives off
those same rays so I figure it zapped my hearing
aid. Anyhow, I got the thing replaced and I still
heard the knocking. Harwin says it's the transmission, but I think he's full of baloney—" *Beeppp*.

The message cut off and went to the next.

"Deanie, honey? Are you there? Pick up if
you're there. I think we got cut off…"

Deanie listened to the rest of the message and
tried to ignore the guilt that churned inside of her,
along with a strange sense of longing. As much as

Deanie wanted to leave the past behind, there were some parts she wished she could take with her.

A breeze blew through the open lobby and teased the edges of her cover-up. Her skin prickled and she became acutely aware of how little she wore and how out of place she suddenly felt.

Not for long, she reminded herself, as she stashed her cell phone and pushed to her feet. She would get the hang of all this girlie stuff if it was the last thing she did. She had no reason to feel self-conscious. Women wore skimpy clothes all the time. Even more, all the important parts were covered.

Sort of.

Her footsteps faltered and she stiffened.

Don't be a wimp. You can *do this.*

She drew a deep breath, pulled back her shoulders and tried to remember everything her Grandma Jilly had taught her during the few summers together that Deanie had been old enough to remember. Their last one, in particular, when she'd been five.

Grandma Jilly had still been grief-stricken at the loss of her only child and all the more determined to maintain a female influence in her young granddaughter's life. That summer they'd paraded around with books on their heads, played dress-up, drank tea, baked cookies and laughed.

They'd had so much fun that Deanie had

actually forgotten how much she hated the frilly dresses and hair bows the other little girls wore to kindergarten.

Deanie, on the other hand, dressed in the Little Husky jeans and T-shirts her dad ordered out of the Sears catalog. She'd even stopped hating the fact that Grandma Jilly called her Nadine.

Until she'd gone back home.

She'd walked into her house wearing a pink dress trimmed in ribbon rosebuds she and Grandma Jilly had spent hours making, white patent leather Mary Jane's and pink lace socks, and her brothers had laughed.

Correction, they'd snorted and bellowed and teased her mercilessly. Needless to say, she'd punched Cory—the oldest and the loudest—in the arm, threatened Clay and Colby and glared at the rest before stomping to her room. She'd changed into her boots, jeans and her favorite John Deere T-shirt, hidden the girlie get-up in the back of her closet, and that had been the end of Nadine.

Until now.

She pulled back her shoulders, held her head up and her body straight, and said a silent prayer to Grandma Jilly to please, *please* smile down on her.

Obviously, the old woman was feeling gracious. While the walk through the lobby and out to the pool seemed endless, she finally made it with a few minutes to spare.

Escapades attracted a predominantly adult clientele made up of mostly couples. Thanks to tomorrow's holiday, there didn't seem to be a single in sight. Pairs gathered at the swim-up bar, others clustered under the massive umbrellas situated here and there. More soaked up the sun side-by-side in various lounge chairs crowded near the shallow end of the pool where a couples' event— a tropical version of the classic *Newlywed Game* being sponsored by a local radio station—was about to take place.

A large table nearby overflowed with fresh fruit and a double-heart ice sculpture to keep everything cool. An upbeat reggae love song poured from the speakers. Beyond the green hedges and brilliant orange hibiscus, the sun shimmered over a turquoise ocean. Palm trees dotted the white-sand beach and swayed with the faint island breeze. The smell of suntan oil and fresh fruit and relationship nirvana teased her nostrils.

Deanie ignored the urge to turn and head back up to her room. So what if she didn't have a significant other? She never would have one if she didn't keep her feet rooted to the spot and her mind on the business at hand—Rance and sex.

Sex and *Rance*.

Her fingers trembled as she held a hand above her eyes to ease the glare.

No familiar beat-up cowboy hat. No hot, tanned body wearing an old T-shirt and board shorts. No killer smile or sparkling eyes.

"Landsakes, child, you're going to kill yourself in those shoes," said a familiar voice.

Deanie turned to see Mavoreen Rosenbaum sitting in a nearby lounge chair. She wore an old-fashioned black, cover-everything-up swimsuit that made her white skin look even whiter. A large straw hat rested atop her head and a huge dab of white sunscreen sat on her prominent nose. A pair of white pool shoes completed the outfit.

Deanie walked over to the woman. Or, at least she tried. But the concrete was ridged and so she wobbled more than she walked. Mavoreen reached up and gave her a steadying hand just as she reached the lounge chair.

"Careful now, or you'll break a leg. A damn shame what women suffer in the name of fashion."

"I'm not used to them. They're new. And so am I. I don't usually dress like this. I mean, I do. Now."

"What's the occasion?"

"I'm starting a new job and I thought I'd get a new look to go with it."

"Good for you." Mavoreen reached up and patted Deanie's arm before her gaze drank in the silk cover-up that concealed Deanie's skimpy swimsuit. "Did you get that at the gift shop? Why, I might just pop in there and see if they've got that in my size. Mitchell would love it. Of course, he won't be seeing it until tomorrow on account of he had a really pressing business meeting he had to tend to."

Deanie couldn't help but remember Savannah's comment. *"There is no billionaire. It's a story she makes up so she doesn't look like a lonely old woman."*

"Ordinarily, I wouldn't tolerate his tardiness," Mavoreen continued, "but he's just so in-tune with the real me. Do you know that he sent me a singing telegram to tell me he wouldn't make it until tomorrow. A Frank Sinatra look-alike." When Deanie didn't seem to make the connection between thoughtful and Frank, Mavoreen added, "The first song we danced to was a Frank Sinatra song. Now there's a man who pays attention to the details and knows there's more to me than just a great body."

"Excuse me, ma'am," a waiter said as he stopped next to Deanie. He smiled at Mavoreen. "We've just had a shift change and Peter, your previous waiter, is off duty. My name is Raoul and it would be my pleasure to serve you."

"Of course it would be, sonny." She gave Deanie a *"What can I do? They just won't leave me alone"* look and shrugged. "Margarita?" she asked Deanie, holding up her own half-emtpy glass.

"Nothing for me," Deanie said. "I really have to go. I'm meeting someone."

"Well, have fun then." Mavoreen waved before turning to the waiter and ordering a refill.

Deanie glanced around again for Rance before resuming her trek around the pool.

Her gaze lit on a vacant lounge chair on the far side of the pool, the deep end, that had been practically abandoned thanks to the radio station who now had the crowd jam-packed in the shallow area.

Picking her way past half-naked bodies and a maze of chairs, she finally reached the remote blue and white striped canvas chaise. It was a tri-fold chair recently vacated by a sun worshipper who'd been stretched out prone.

Deanie spent a few seconds looking for some sort of switch that would let her bend the back into an upright position. While she knew she and Rance would get prone eventually, she was through being the pushy, anxious sort she'd been as a teenager.

He owed her, and so she wasn't going to make his penance any easier by being in the right position, even if it was the wrong time and place.

She couldn't find the lever to bend the chair back into position. Finally, she gave up and sank onto the middle section. She slipped off the strappy sandals and stretched her legs out in front of her. She'd just reached for her sunscreen when she heard the deep, familiar rumble of Rance's voice.

6

"YOU LOOK REALLY HOT." Rance's deep voice echoed in Deanie's ears and sent a burst of heat through her. Her breath caught for a long moment before she remembered to breathe.

She squinted up at the large shadow that he made outlined by the bright sunlight. "There were no umbrellas on this end of the pool and there wasn't a place to sit over there." She pointed to the far side where a crowd clustered near the shallow end of the gigantic pool. A makeshift tent had been set up. Inside, three separate tables hosted three different couples. A local radio disc jockey was playing host. "I had no choice but to sit here and cook."

He grinned. "I mean *hot* as in good looking."

"Oh." Duh.

"Did you pick that dress out after I left?"

"It's not a dress. It's a swimsuit cover-up." She made a big show of smoothing the skirt material over her thighs, all the while trying to calm her suddenly racing heart.

"You're at the pool. You don't need a cover-up."

"Not now, but I just got here. On the way, I needed a cover-up."

Yeah, right.

There were near-naked bodies all over the hotel. Deanie just wasn't in a hurry to be one of them.

"Besides," she added, "I thought this would be a good chance to break it in."

"Don't you do that with shoes instead of clothes?"

"Some material can be itchier than others," she retorted, wishing the material in question didn't feel so silky and smooth and rousing against her palms. "It's better to know early on, that way you can take it back before the return period expires or wash it with a fabric softener."

His eyes glittered like whiskey pools and she plunged right in and sank to the bottom for a long, heart-pounding moment.

"So is it?" he finally asked, his deep voice jerking her back to the surface.

"Is it what?"

"Itchy?"

"Not really."

"Then you can take it off." He hooked a leg over the chair and straddled the chaise behind her before she could draw her next breath. His thighs framed hers and his chest cushioned her back. His hands settled on her shoulders for a long, breathless moment before tracing her upper arms.

"You feel hot, too."

"The sun."

"Maybe." His lips touched the shell of her ear. "And maybe not." His hands stopped at her elbows before sliding back up over her shoulders. Strong fingers lifted the hair away from her neck. She felt the cool rush of fresh air followed by the hot press of his lips.

"What are you doing?"

"Following the Camp E.D.E.N. curriculum and the first workshop—Shedding Your Inhibitions."

"Shouldn't we find someplace a little more private? With less people?"

"We could, but that would defeat the whole purpose of the workshop. *Shedding your inhibitions* is all about tuning everything else out and tuning in to yourself. If you can focus enough to do that here, now, with all of these people, then you'll ace this topic and be that much closer to your goal."

To you and me and sex.

The words played through her head before she could stop them and remember that her ultimate goal was to get in touch with her inner sexuality and unleash the vixen within.

Sex with Rance was just a means to an end—a new Deanie—not the end itself.

A hip-swaying calypso tune livened up the group at the far end of the pool. A roar of laughter went up from the crowd. Waiters darted here and there near the commotion. A world away, it seemed, from where they sat. At the same time, they were still in plain view should anyone happen to turn.

"I still don't think—"

"Don't think," he cut in. His lips nuzzled her ear. "Just take this off." He tugged at the knot she'd made just over one shoulder. "And let's get on with the lesson."

RANCE EXPECTED one of two things when he touched Deanie. That she would 1) forget her stubbornness, morph into her old self and jump his bones or 2) harden her resolve and keep up her cold, aloof front.

Either way, both were *her* reactions.

Rance didn't anticipate the fierceness of his own need and the near uncontrollable urge to pull her around, push her down and press himself into her hot, tight body. His breath caught as her heat seeped into his fingertips and zigzagged straight to his crotch. His cock twitched and his balls ached and his hands actually started to tingle.

Deprivation, he told himself. He hadn't been with a woman in months because he'd been on the mend at the Iron Horse. It only stood to reason that he'd go a little nuts when he finally got up close and personal with a female. Even if the female were Teeny Deanie Codge.

Because it was Deanie.

Because he'd thought about her more than once since that night on the riverbank.

The truth echoed through his head as fiercely as the want vibrated through his body. He *had* thought about her. Many times. Too many for a man who'd vowed to leave the past behind and forget everything and everybody. He'd meant to start fresh. To bury the hurt and the pain of his memories once and for all and think only of the future.

The next game.

The next competition.

But try as he might, he'd never completely forgotten Deanie. She'd been the one person who'd made him smile, and the only person who'd made him think twice about leaving Romeo all those years ago.

Because he'd felt something for her. Friendship and like and lust.

He'd recognized the first two when they'd been

just kids, even if he'd never admitted as much to her. She'd known. She'd seen it in his smile. Hell, she'd seen it in his frown when he'd been hurting over his parents' deaths. He'd told her to get lost, but she'd known he'd really wanted her there. He'd needed her, and so she'd stayed.

The lust…

He'd hadn't recognized that until the night she'd offered herself to him and he'd had the nearly overwhelming urge to cross the few feet of distance between them and kiss her for all he was worth.

He'd wanted to.

Hell, he'd wanted *her.* So much that it had hurt.

But he'd seen her heart in her eyes and he'd known that taking her then and there would have meant taking a lot more than just her sweet, delectable body.

Deanie had fancied herself in love with him. She'd wanted a happily ever after, and there'd been no such thing in the cards for Rance. When Rance's father had died, his grandfather had taken over the ranch. He'd assumed responsibility for Rance and his brothers, as well, but he hadn't wanted them around. They'd reminded the old man of the son he'd lost and so he'd pushed his grandsons away. Rance had given up steer wrestling and spent his extra time practicing with his high school football team as their star tackle. Before long, he'd been on his way out of town, away from the ranch and the old man who'd stopped loving him and his brothers.

He'd been *this* close to gone that night, and so he'd only been in the position to give her a few blissful moments.

And now?

It didn't matter what he could or couldn't give her. She'd made it crystal clear that she didn't want anything from him, least of all a long-term relationship.

No cuddling in front of the TV every night. No sharing breakfast, lunch or dinner down at the Fat Cow Diner. No lazing around together on Sunday afternoons or dusting the floor at Romeo's one and only honky tonk on Saturday night.

She had plans that didn't include him.

The truth bothered him a hell of a lot more than it should have, considering the fact that Rance didn't want a long-term relationship with anyone. His lifestyle was much too unsettled.

Which meant he should be pleased with Deanie's sudden about face.

Should be? To hell with that. He *was* pleased. Happy. *Ecstatic*.

He fought down the irritation that niggled at his

gut. He damned sure didn't want her to want an ongoing relationship with him. He just wanted her to want him, period. To admit it. To *act* on it.

Rance focused on his throbbing cock and the woman perched between his legs. The wrap she'd had knotted securely around her had come loose and now pooled at her waist, effectively hiding the erection that strained beneath his shorts and pushed against her soft, round ass.

Drawing a deep breath, he let his gaze travel the smooth, pale expanse of her back. The thin straps of her bikini top knotted just below her shoulder blades.

Rance fought back the urge to trace the straps around her rib cage and slide his hands beneath the skimpy material barely concealing her full, lush breasts. He wanted to touch her bare nipples, to feel them ripen with need.

The same need that coursed through his own body and made his muscles bunch.

But he knew he had to pace himself, to keep his cool and launch a full blown attack on her senses. It was all about breaching her line of defense, tackling every barrier and turning her on beyond the point of no return.

Until she wanted him so much that she gladly offered herself up the way she had that night.

He gathered his control, let loose a deep, shaky

breath and reached into her partially open bag that sat next to the chair. Retrieving her sunscreen, he opened the tube and dribbled the white cream along the curve of one silky smooth shoulder, and then the other.

"Hold your hair up," he murmured, his lips grazing her ear. She visibly trembled and his gut tightened.

Rance drew a deep breath, gathered every ounce of control that he possessed and touched her.

SHE KNEW he was going to touch her.

It wasn't like he was just going to squeeze the sunscreen onto her and then up and leave. Of course, he was going to work it into her skin. *Massage* it in. Slowly and thoroughly.

She knew that. Just as she knew his hands would be large and strong and warm. The way she'd imagined whenever she replayed their one night so long ago and fantasized a much different ending. One where he actually reached out rather than running away from her.

But her imagination didn't begin to do him justice. His hands were even larger than she'd thought. Stronger. And forget warm. They were hot. Scorching.

His long fingers closed over her shoulders and

her breath caught. A steamy heat radiated from the point of contact and swept along her nerve endings, burning up everything in its wake. Her determination. Her resistance. Her common sense.

She tried to sit up straight, to concentrate on the sparkling pool that stretched out in front of her and the cluster of people at the opposite end. But the only thing she could think of was the man who sat behind her, surrounding her, consuming her.

His deep, even breaths filled her ears. His rich, mesmerizing scent teased her nostrils. The rough feel of his strong, callused hands stirred every nerve as they slid over her shoulders, down her arms and back up again. His muscular thighs framed hers, his deep tan making her skin look almost white in comparison. But in a good way. She felt small compared to him. Soft. Fair. *Feminine.*

More so when he pulled her bottom back more firmly into the cradle of his thighs. His groin pressed into her buttocks and awareness bolted through her. He was hard. Very hard.

The realization stirred an ache between her legs and she had the sudden urge to turn and rub her crotch up against his.

As soon as the thought struck, she stiffened. She would fling herself headfirst into the pool before she let that happen.

"Close your eyes," he murmured. His voice slid into her ear and sent a tingle of awareness to her nipples. "You're too tense. You need to stop thinking about everyone else."

"I'm not thinking about everyone else."

"Then what are you thinking about?"

"That I should move."

"If you do that, darlin', it's only going to get harder." For emphasis, he moved. Just a momentary press of his groin against her buttocks, but it was enough. He seemed to grow bigger. His weight strained more fully against her bottom and she caught her breath.

"I meant that maybe I should move away," she managed to say after several frantic heartbeats. *Now. Right now.*

"That would mean giving in to your inhibitions, not shedding them. You're uptight because we're in a public place and there are dozens of people who could very easily glance our way at any moment."

If only.

"To strip away your inhibitions," he instructed, "you have to do the opposite of what your brain tells you." He said the words slowly, each one loaded with promise. "If your head tells you to move, you stay right…" He pulled her more firmly against him, her back flush against his chest "…here."

His hands slid down her arms to the cover-up, the edges puddled in her lap. He pulled the material free, letting it slide from between them, and dropped it on the ground next to her bag.

Deanie felt a rush of self-consciousness at sitting there wearing nothing but her skimpy bikini, Rance straddling the seat behind her. But then he dribbled sunscreen onto one bare thigh and her brain short-circuited.

7

THE COOL, CREAMY LIQUID oozed over Deanie's hot skin as he moved to squeeze more onto her other thigh. Her heart pounded as he set the bottle to the side and touched her, his hands on either thigh, and started to smooth the lotion.

Strong, purposeful fingers rubbed circles into her skin, moving along the outside of her legs, higher to where her swimsuit rode high on her hips. He paused at the edge before tracing the line down toward the bottom of the vee. She stiffened, her heart pounding so loudly in her ears that she almost didn't hear the low, deep, rumble of his voice.

"You like that, don't you?"

"I…" she stammered, but then one fingertip grazed the material covering her pubic area, as if his hand had accidentally slipped from its original purpose, and the answer collided into a jumble at the back of her throat.

"Think about how much you like it and stop worrying about who might be watching."

But she wasn't worrying about who might have seen the intimate touch. She was more worried about whether or not he would do it again.

About how much she *wanted* him to do it again.

He slid his palms over her thighs toward her knees and back up, his thumbs grazing the seam where her legs met before separating and moving to the outside of her thighs and back up again. And then he repeated the process.

Again.

And again.

Electricity threaded through her body and tightened. She felt the pull in her nipples and between her legs. Her lungs constricted and she couldn't seem to drag enough air into them.

"You like this, don't you?"

She nodded. She liked the way he touched her, so hungry and desperate, as if he couldn't get enough of her. She liked the way he made her feel so restless and hungry inside, as if she couldn't get enough of him.

She liked *him.*

"You want me to keep touching you, don't you?"

She drew a shaky breath and nodded again.

"What if I told you that someone was watching us?"

"Is there someone?"

"Does it matter? Would you really want me to stop? Or would you want me to touch you anyway?"

"I…" She drew a sharp breath as his fingertip slid beneath the edge of her bikini bottom and traced the seam between her legs. "I want you to touch me anyway. *Because*."

Because the notion that someone would see him touch her, desire her, would make it that much more real.

She'd had such a deep crush on him way back when and she'd desperately wanted him to return her feelings. She'd imagined it time and time again. She'd mistaken his smile every morning when she'd climbed onto the school bus for interest. Misinterpreted him saying hello in the hallway at school for genuine like. Labeled innocent acts of kindness—such as when she'd forgotten her lunch and he'd given her his or the time he'd asked her to dance at the Elks Lodge fund-raiser because she'd been the only one without a date—as surefire signs of attraction.

She'd fooled herself until the truth had stared her baldly in the face. There'd been no way to sugarcoat his rejection that night at the lake. He'd walked right by her, straight into the water, and it had been obvious that he'd felt nothing for her.

Back then.

But now?

The fingertip parting her folds, plying the soft, slick tissue, wasn't a figment of her overactive imagination. No carefully constructed fantasy. No wet dream in the dead of night.

The touch was real. He was real. And he really wanted her.

As much as she wanted him.

Just as the thought struck, she forced it back out. This wasn't about wanting *him*. It was about wanting, pure and simple. About tuning in to her own body and focusing solely on the way her heart beat and her skin tingled.

She told herself that over the next few moments as he dipped inside her steamy heat and her body seemed to tighten around him. Pressure pulled inside of her, winding tight as he pressed deeper. Once. Twice. Each probe took her breath away, the sensation sharper, sweeter, but it wasn't enough. She needed more. She moved her hips, begging him deeper, but he didn't oblige. Instead, he withdrew until his touch rested between her slick folds, as if he waited for her to grab him and pull him back inside.

She fought the urge and took advantage of his retreat to drag some much needed air into her deflated lungs.

"Have you ever had an orgasm like this? With just a man's hand between your legs? Moving back and forth? Up and down?" The rough pad of his finger slid between her lush lips until he brushed her clitoris.

Pleasure, so fierce and intense, pierced her brain and shattered her resistance for a heart-stopping moment.

"Have you?" His deep voice slid past the thunder of her own heartbeat.

"I…" She licked her lips.

"Tell me."

No. The word was there on the tip of her tongue, but she clamped her lips shut and kept it from going any farther. She bolted to her feet.

"Deanie?" He followed her to where she stood trying to catch her breath by the pool. "What's wrong?"

"Nothing." She drew some much needed air into her legs and summoned her best smile. "Mission accomplished."

"What are you talking about?"

"The first workshop. I passed. I let you touch

me in a public place and I managed to push every-thing aside and focus on the way it made me feel."

"Which was?"

"Nice."

"Nice?"

"Good." She tried to look nonchalant. "Pretty good."

"I felt you tighten around me." His deep, seduc-tive voice slid into her ears and stirred her already throbbing body. "I *know* it felt better."

"Okay, so it felt better than good." He arched an eyebrow and before she could stop herself, she blurted, "It felt great." When he grinned, she added, "But great is a far cry from spectacular. And it didn't feel spectacular. Not *orgasmic* spectacular."

His expression hardened. "It would have if you hadn't jumped up like that."

"Maybe." She shrugged. "And maybe not."

His gaze narrowed dangerously. "Are you saying you weren't going to have an orgasm?"

The way he said the last word caused a bolt of desire that struck right between her legs. Her thighs clenched and she cleared her suddenly dry throat. "I—I might have—" She licked her lips "—but the odds are just as great that I wouldn't have."

She'd been close. So close. But he didn't know that and she wasn't going to tell him because that would mean admitting that he could make her feel things no other man ever had.

That he was different. Special.

Her one and only.

He wasn't, she told herself for the umpteenth time. The thing was, with him so close and so masculine and so downright sexy, she was having more and more trouble believing it. And when he stared at her with that knowing light in his whiskey-colored eyes, she flat out didn't buy it at all.

Even more, she knew he didn't buy it. He saw past her defenses to the trembling, panting, needy woman beneath, and damned if he didn't smile—a slow tilt to his sensuous lips that made her want to kiss him, long and slow and deep, almost as much as she wanted to hold on to her pride.

Almost.

"Look me in the eyes and tell me you didn't just have one of the most amazing times of your life."

She caught and held his gaze. *Do it,* she told herself. *Tell him before you lose your nerve. Or worse, before you up and kiss him.*

She wasn't going to kiss him. She had willpower.

Unless he grinned at her, that is. Then she wouldn't be able to help herself.

He grinned. "You can't say it, can you?"

"No, but let's see if you understand hand

gestures." She reached out and shoved for all she was worth. It was that or kiss him, and Deanie wasn't making the same mistake twice. She'd put her pride on the line once before for Rance McGraw and he'd stomped all over it.

He wasn't rejecting her this time.

"WHAT THE…" *hell* drowned in a mouthful of water as Rance slammed into the deep end and went under. He came up sputtering a few seconds later and glared up at Deanie who stood near the edge of the pool, an unreadable expression on her face.

"Dammit, woman! What was that for?"

"You seemed a little hot around the collar and I thought you needed to cool off."

"By drowning me?"

"If memory serves me, you're a better than average swimmer."

"Not with a concussion. I damned near hit the bottom of the pool."

Deanie fought back a wave of compassion and held tight to the sudden surge of anger that rushed through her, along with her memories.

"I never figured you for the careful type, what with wrangling snakes and all that other stuff you do in the name of sports."

"They *are* sports. *Extreme* sports."

"*Extremely* nutty sports. Then again, you've never been one to use good judgment. What were you thinking jumping into that lake at midnight while you were three sheets to the wind?" The question was out before she could stop it. "You could have killed yourself."

But then death had been preferable to a hot night with Deanie Codge, her bruised ego whispered.

"Yeah, well that *was* stupid." His voice was quiet, laced with an unmistakable regret. As he stared up into her eyes, Deanie had the distinct suspicion that he was talking about more than just jumping into the lake. And then he opened his mouth, and his words confirmed the feeling. "I did a lot of stupid things that night." His gaze darkened and sincerity glimmered in the dark golden depths. "I shouldn't have turned you down, Deanie."

"Yeah, well…" She'd rehearsed this moment in her dreams so many times back then when she'd been so hurt. He'd said he was sorry and she'd proceeded to tell him what a low-life scumbag he was. He'd hurt her and so she'd wanted to hurt him. But now, with the regret swimming in his eyes, she couldn't seem to find the words.

"I—I think I hear my cell phone ringing." She turned and rushed back to the lounge chair, and snatched up her bag. Behind her, water splashed as Rance moved toward the edge of the pool.

"Yep, it's my phone, all right." Or it would have been if she'd left the thing turned on. "I really should get back inside where it's quiet and return the call. It's probably Calvin, or maybe Miss Geneva back home. Her radiator just won't behave itself." She grabbed her discarded wrap, snatched up her shoes and started around the pool just as water sloshed and Rance hauled himself onto the concrete.

She ignored the urge to look and picked up her steps. Not because she feared him coming after her. But because she feared flinging herself into his arms if he did. An urge she knew would be that much stronger if she chanced a glance behind her and saw him standing there dripping wet, his board shorts clinging to him like a second skin. She'd imagined what he'd looked like more than once after he'd climbed out of the lake all those years ago. Of course, she'd imagined years later, after the initial hurt had faded and she'd traded her young girl daydreams for a woman's erotic fantasies.

Fantasies, mind you. But this was reality and it was much more complicated.

"I shouldn't have turned you down."

The admission echoed in her head and sent a burst of joy through her. Not satisfaction or a sense of justice. But *joy*. As in, she still cared. As in, she still *felt* for him.

She did.

But the emotion driving her now was pure lust. He'd worked her up on the lounge chair and she was in desperate need of a really good orgasm. It only stood to reason that she would be close to jumping his bones right now.

It didn't have anything to do with the fact that he really and truly regretted rejecting her that night.

She ignored the strange flutter in her chest and concentrated on the way her nipples tingled and her thighs clenched with each step.

Because this day—twenty hours left and counting—was all about sex.

It wasn't about whether or not she still liked Rance. She wasn't a naive girl. She knew now what she'd been too young to understand then— they couldn't have had a future together. He'd been a man hell-bent on running from home and she'd been a woman intent on having one. She wanted a happily ever after, and Rance was only interested in the next twenty-four hours. Even if he now wanted her, it was only in the physical sense. He didn't share her hopes and dreams.

He didn't *love* her.

He never had.

Relief washed through her when she made it several steps without him dogging her, along with a strange sense of disappointment.

She shook away the feeling. While she was very close to exploding from sexual frustration, she wasn't crazy from it. Not yet.

"Meet me in the lobby in an hour for the next workshop," he called out just as she rounded the far edge of the pool.

Excitement bubbled, along with joy. The same pure, unadulterated joy she'd felt just moments ago.

Ugh. So much for *not yet.* She was crazy, all right.

But she wasn't stupid.

RANCE WATCHED DEANIE disappear around a large group of potted palms and mentally recited every Pro-Rodeo steer wrestling champion for the past twenty years.

He wasn't sure why. He should have had alligator wrangling on the brain right now. But it only seemed fitting for him to think of steer wrestling when it came to Deanie. Partly because she reminded him of his past when he'd loved the sport, and partly because he itched to stomp after her, wrestle her down and take her then and there, the crowd gathered around the bar area be damned.

But he wouldn't go that far. He would push her

to the edge, but she had to jump over willingly. Because she wanted to. Because she wanted him.

He focused on the thought, walked over to the lounge chair and picked up his discarded shirt. He wiped the moisture from his eyes and scrubbed at his hair before hooking the soft cotton around his neck. He should have dried off, but at the moment, he needed the cool water drip-dropping down his hot, tight skin before he headed inside to meet Erica and see if she'd come up with a list of the island's most romantic spots. If he intended to seduce Deanie, he needed something special for the next workshop. Different. Seductive.

His groin throbbed at the thought and he shook his head as he slid his feet into his flip-flops. Despite a thorough soaking in the pool, he was still worked up. Hot. Hard. *Shaking,* for Christ's sake.

Why, he hadn't been this desperate since…

An image rushed at him as he started for the hotel lobby. He remembered the two mile trek home once Deanie had left and he'd climbed from the lake that night. He'd been soaking wet and the night air had been chilly, but neither had been enough to cool the fire that had burned in his gut. He'd gone home, straight past his suitcases that were packed and sitting in the hallway, and into a cold shower. Then he'd crawled into bed and tried to sleep.

Instead, he'd tossed and turned and thought about her the rest of the night. And then he'd packed her memory away the next morning, along with the rest of his past, said goodbye to his brothers—his grandfather had been out riding fence and hadn't been the least bit interested in seeing him off—and he'd left for the rest of his life.

Just as he would do tomorrow once he'd gotten Deanie out of his system and spent the lust raging inside him.

Oddly enough, he didn't feel any more excited about the prospect now than he'd felt back then.

8

DEANIE STEPPED onto the crowded elevator and punched the button for the fourteenth floor. She wobbled toward the rear of the elevator—the best she could manage since her feet had launched a full-blown rebellion against the new high heels. She clutched the wrap around her shoulders with one hand and her bag in the other. Leaning back against the far wall, she tried to calm her pounding heart.

Not because of what Rance had said, she reminded herself for the umpteenth time. She was still so worked up and excited because she'd seen him dripping wet.

It was all just physical. About the sex.

The elevator stopped and she glanced to see that they'd reached the third floor. Several people got off and the remaining passengers shifted to give each other some breathing room. The doors slid shut and the elevator continued it's trek upward.

Deanie ignored the hollow feel in her stomach

that had nothing to do with the elevator car and everything to do with her encounter with Rance.

Her very close encounter.

She still couldn't believe she'd gotten up close and personal with *Rance,* of all people. She'd dreamed of it so many times, built him up in her head to be some super lover that it was a wonder she hadn't been disappointed. Everyone knew fantasy was always better than reality.

Not in this case.

The real Rance had been a thousand times better. The feel of his skin had been hotter. The touch of his hand more purposeful. His body had felt more muscular and overwhelmingly powerful pressed up against her. He'd smelled richer and more intoxicating. His voice had even sounded huskier and sexier and more sincere than she'd ever imagined when he'd said—

She derailed the last thought, shut her eyes and concentrated on picturing him wet.

Water dripped down his bare torso. Trickling through his dark chest hair. His skin glistening. His eyes gleaming with desire and that flash of regret—

Wait a second.

She rearranged her thoughts, bypassed the whole regret thing and forced her attention down the very vivid mental image she'd managed to conjure.

Mmm… *He had great abs. Solid. Rippled. Bisected by a funnel of dark, silky hair that disappeared into the waistband of his shorts.*

Dinggg!

The elevator stopped again and Deanie glanced up to note that they'd reached the fifth floor. More people climbed out and a few climbed back on.

The doors slid closed, the elevator moved on and Deanie returned to her mental speculation.

She'd been at the waistband, following the line of his zipper down…

Dinggg!

They hit the eighth floor and the rest of the passengers stepped off. A man wearing a white fluffy robe and flip-flops stepped on.

Now where was she? Oh, yeah. She'd been tracing the zipper over a very impressive bulge. Her cheeks burned, but she forced her mind to continue, to imagine what lay beneath the material. She had no doubt that it would be a very substantial package.

Dinggg!

Definitely bigger than the package dangling right in front of her—

She blinked once, twice, but it didn't disappear. She forced her gaze upward, but it was too late. The man turned and darted off the elevator before she could glimpse his face, the white robe trailing from his hand as he streaked buck-naked down the tenth floor hallway.

"Could you tell me the man's size?"

Deanie smoothed the edge of the gray T-shirt she'd pulled on, along with matching sweatpants, before rushing downstairs to the hotel security office to report the naked man incident.

"Well." She nibbled on her bottom lip as she gave the question some serious thought. "I didn't have a ruler, but I'd say he was maybe four of five inches."

"Not his penis size, Miss Codge." Mr. H., the head of security at Escapades, gave her an exasperated look. He was a large, muscular man—minus any visible hair—who looked like a cross between Aladdin's genie and Mr. Clean. He wore Chinos and enough gold chains around his thick neck to decrease the national deficit by a nice chunk. "His build," he continued. "Was he a small man? Medium? Large?"

"Oh. Um, of course." Deanie's cheeks burned and she shifted in the leather chair where she sat in front of a massive chrome and glass desk.

Windows lined one wall, giving a spectacular view of a lush garden area surrounded by a sparkling pond being fed by a massive waterfall. Small round tables covered with crisp white linens sat here and there amid the green foliage and colorful tropical flowers. Large, fat candles glittered from the center of each table. A rainbow of spotlights played across the sparkling water.

"I, um, didn't really get an overall picture of him."

"Because you were too busy staring at his penis," the security manager said matter-of-factly, shifting forward, his large frame effectively blocking her view of The Falls, the one of a kind restaurant the cab driver had mentioned.

Deanie gave him her *best back-off-buddy* look. "I wouldn't call it *staring,* at least not by choice. One minute I had my eyes closed and the next, the elevator buzzed. My eyes opened and there it was, hanging right in front of me. I couldn't help but look."

Yeah, right his gaze seemed to say. It took all of her control to keep her fingers from balling into a fist. She wasn't ten years old anymore. She didn't have to come up swinging to be taken seriously. She was all grown up. An ultra-femme woman in control of her own destiny.

Her fingers brushed the soft cotton edge of the sexless T-shirt. Okay, so maybe she wasn't ultra-femme at the moment. But she was in control. And she wasn't going to lose her cool and go postal on a man twice her size. Even one who was annoying as hell.

"Hanging." He seemed to think before making several notes on his pad. "Meaning it wasn't erect?"

"No. That is, I don't think so." She shook her head. "What difference does it make?"

"It helps us to know what we're dealing with. Is this a harmless exhibitionist—someone who craves attention—or is this someone who gets sexually excited by showing off his goods?" He made a few more notes before tapping his pencil on the edge of the desk. His gaze met hers. "Do you remember anything else about the perpetrator? Other than the fact that he was flaccid?"

"I…" She conjured the image. "He was old," she declared after a few thoughtful moments.

"How do you know?"

"He had gray hair." She studied the mental picture still vivid in her head. "I guess it could be premature gray. My oldest brother had his first gray hair at twenty-two. He's in his thirties and completely salt and pepper now."

Mr. H. gave her an exasperated look. "But I thought you didn't see the perpetrator's face…" Understanding finally lit his expression and he grunted what sounded like "Oh."

"And a saggy butt," Deanie added. "I saw that

part when he was jogging away. I guess that would mean he wasn't prematurely gray. He had to be old." She conjured the image again. "Then again, he could just be out of shape. That would bring us back to the premature gray conclusion."

"Maybe." The security guard made several more notes before leaning back in his chair and eyeing her for several moments. "You're absolutely sure it was a male?" he finally asked. "There's no chance that it could be a woman?"

"No."

"You're positive?"

"Of course. I saw…" It flashed in her mind again and her face burned that much hotter. "Well, you know what I saw." She swallowed. "It was definitely a male. Maybe an old male, or just an out-of-shape male with premature gray. Either way, it was a man."

He gave her a speculative glance before his attention dropped to the notepad. He flipped through several pages and shook his head. "I know you're sure of what you saw, Miss Codge, but to be honest, it simply doesn't fit with the other reports we've had today."

"He's done it before?"

"Not he. *She*. We've had three sightings involving a female perpetrator in the past two hours. An elderly woman with gray hair was spotted out by the pool. And again down on the beach."

Deanie thought a second. "I'm sorry, but he was definitely a he. Unless it was a really good prosthetic. Then again, wouldn't she have had breasts?" She shook her head. "I'm sure I would have noticed breasts." Pretty sure. But he/she *had* caught her off guard. "It happened really fast."

"These things always do." He pushed to his feet and walked around the desk. "Thank you for coming in." He shook her hand.

Deanie stood. "I wish I'd had more time. Not to look at his you-know-what," she blurted. "To look at everything else."

"We'll be sure to notify you if we find him. Her. It." He shook his head. "I hope this hasn't ruined your vacation."

"Actually, that took a bad turn long before the elevator incident." The moment, in fact, that she'd spotted Rance McGraw on her flight out of San Antonio.

That's what common sense told her.

Along with the advice that she should abandon the workshops with Rance and just bide her time. She only had eighteen hours until she boarded the plane for Eden. It wasn't as if she was missing all that much. Only a few classes. She could easily borrow someone's notes or ask for a handout. She didn't really *need* Rance's instruction.

Ah, but she wanted it and so she couldn't shake the anxiety that gripped her because the clock was ticking, the minutes slipping away.

She picked up her steps as she left the security office and headed back up to her room to change for their meeting down in the lobby.

She'd just stepped off the elevator on her floor—all the while giving thanks that she'd avoided any naked men along the way—when she spotted Rance at the far end of the hallway.

He leaned against the wall that faced her door, his arms folded and his beat-up straw Resistol tipped low. He wore his usual flip-flops and a new pair of blue-and-white flower-print board shorts that hung low on his trim waist. A crisp white T-shirt hugged his shoulders and arms and created a stark contrast against his tanned skin. Her heart revved into overdrive and her body went on red alert.

She became instantly aware of the soft cotton that covered her torso and the plastic flip-flops that cushioned her sore feet.

Great. Friggin' great.

What was wrong with her? She should have put on her new sundress and heels before going to the security office. And some makeup. And she definitely should have done something with her hair besides pulling it back into a ponytail.

But she'd been in a hurry to report the incident and so she hadn't had time to even glance in the mirror, much less worry over her appearance. She'd pulled on the first thing she'd seen—the T-shirt and sweats she'd purchased during her rush of insecurity down in the gift shop—and had headed back downstairs.

Okay, so maybe she'd spotted the sundress first, but she'd been freaked out and in desperate need of something comfortable.

Familiar.

Her memory stirred and she saw herself standing on the sidelines after a Friday night football game. She'd been waiting for Rance to come off the field so that she could congratulate him on another win. She'd seen him and waved, but he hadn't looked past the handful of cheerleaders—with their long legs and tiny waists and perky breasts—that lingered near the fifty yard line.

Deanie had been twelve then and not the least bit interested in having breasts, period, much less perky ones. The one and only training bra her father had bought for her itched like crazy and so she'd left it stuck in the back of the drawer and worn an undershirt instead.

And that's why he noticed them and not you.

Where the clothes had made her feel oddly secure earlier, she now had the sudden urge to rip them off and burn them before it was too late.

Before he realizes you're still the same old Deanie.

She stiffened at the thought. She wasn't the same. She was different now, even if she didn't look it at that particular moment.

Or feel it.

She shook away the last notion and scrambled for a plan. All she had to do was make a quick escape into her room, wiggle into the sexy dress and slap on some makeup. She would forget all about her momentary lapse into the old Deanie, and so would Rance.

She pulled back her shoulders, pasted on a smile and tried for the sexiest, and fastest walk she could manage in a pair of flip-flops.

The slap-slap of her shoes drew Rance's attention and he turned. His gaze collided with hers as he pushed away from the wall.

"I know I'm late," she said as she came up to him. "Give me ten minutes and I'll meet you downstairs." She grabbed the door handle and pushed her key card into the slot before pulling it back out. The green light on the lock refused to come on and the door remained locked. She tried the card again. Still no green light.

So much for a quick escape.

"What happened?" his deep voice sounded right behind her and she knew he was close. Too close. The hair on the back of her neck prickled and her hands trembled.

"I saw a naked man," she told him as she fed the card into the slot a third time. Or at least she tried.

"A *what?*"

"A naked man. On the elevator." What was it with the stupid key? "At least, I think it was a man." She went for try number four. The door remained locked.

"What did he look like?"

"I don't really know."

"How big was he?"

She was *not* going there again. "I'm not sure. I didn't get a really good look at him." *Come on key,* she prayed. *Work. Please work.* "Just a, um, certain body part."

"You were on the elevator with him and you didn't see anything but his—"

"I was preoccupied," she cut in, whipping the key free and jiggling the door handle.

"Slow down," he murmured a split second before one hand slid around her waist. His other came up to cover hers as she tried to press the key card into the slot yet again. His lips brushed her ear and desire sizzled through her. "You have to slide it in nice and slow if you want a good connection."

With his hard body pressed against hers and his scent surrounding her, scrambling her common sense, the only thing she could think of was him sliding into her. Nice and slow. Again and again.

"I…I'm doing it."

"Not yet," he said, his voice so raw and husky that she knew he was talking about more than just unlocking her door.

He guided her trembling fingers to the slot, eased the card inside and the green light lit.

"Thanks," she murmured as the handle turned and the door opened.

"My pleasure." His lips grazed her ear again and a shiver zigzagged down her spine. "So tell me," he said, making no move to slide his arm free of her waist. "What were you so preoccupied with on the elevator?"

You.

She licked her lips and tried to ignore the warm pull of his body behind her and the press of his hot palm against her stomach. His touch seemed to burn through the thin cotton of her T-shirt…

Ohmigod, the T-shirt.

"Nothing important," she blurted as reality

zapped her and a wave of self-consciousness washed through her.

His arm tightened around her for a heart-stopping moment, as if he meant to question her further, but then his hand fell away and she found herself free.

Deanie gathered her scattered common sense and stepped into the room. "I'll meet you down in the lobby." She turned to close the door on him, but he'd already followed her in.

"I'll wait here." He walked toward the windows that spanned the length of one wall and overlooked the white sand beach. The setting sun bobbed on the horizon and cast an orange glow on the endless stretch of ocean. "You've got a perfect view."

A perfectly romantic view for a couple deeply and desperately in love.

She ignored the burst of longing that went through her at the sudden thought. She didn't love Rance. She didn't want to love him. She just wanted one night with him—*this* night—to ease the sting of rejection she'd felt so long ago and satisfy the lust for him that still kept her up at night.

Turning toward the closet, she busied herself retrieving her outfit. She was about to race into the bathroom to get dressed when her cell phone rang.

She had half a mind not to answer it, but then

she remembered Miss Margie's message and she realized it might be the old woman.

She can leave a message.

She could, but then Deanie would have even more guilt to deal with. She felt bad enough that she'd left her customers to Harwin. She wouldn't make things worse by not answering questions during a time of need.

Besides, she liked Miss Margie.

But if it was anyone else, she wasn't picking up. No way. No how.

She snatched up the cell phone and glanced at the caller ID display. *Judy Louise Eldenheimer*

Okay, so it wasn't Miss Margie. But Deanie liked Miss Judy, too. The old woman had baked the best sugar cookies in town and she'd brought Deanie a baker's dozen each and every time she'd had to bring her car into the shop. Since she'd driven an ancient Buick with a fading transmission, that had been at least once a month. Of course, she'd brought the cookies in lieu of payment, but Deanie hadn't minded. She'd loved those sugar cookies. Even more, she'd loved the way Miss Judy had decorated the cookie box with lots of lace and pearls and frilly ribbon, as if Deanie weren't just a mechanic but a woman who appreciated the prettier things in life. And so

Deanie had gladly accepted the goodies and for-
feited her labor charges. Parts had been a different matter, but she'd given them to Miss Judy at
cost—without Big Daddy's knowledge, of
course—and saved the old woman who'd lived on
a fixed income a small fortune.

Yep, she liked Miss Judy and so she couldn't
help the rush of worry that went through her when
she saw the old woman's name.

She pressed the on button. "Miss Judy? What's
wrong?"

RANCE SANK into a nearby chair and watched
Deanie's expression go from worried to relieved.

"That's nothing to worry over. Tell Harwin to
change the transmission fluid—" Her words
scrambled to a halt as her gaze collided with
Rance's. "Excuse me a second, Miss Judy." She
covered the mouthpiece. "This is sort of private,"
she told Rance as she gathered up her dress and
shoes and the phone. "I'll just be a few minutes."
She fled into the bathroom.

Rance had half a mind to follow her in. Not to
hear her conversation, but to persuade her to
answer his question about what she'd been preoccupied with on the elevator. Had she been
thinking about him? About her near orgasm by the

pool? He had a hunch she had, but he wanted to hear the words.

He needed to hear them.

But following her would put her close again and he wasn't in any hurry to test his already shaky control. It was all about seducing her at this point, not pressing her up against the bathroom wall and driving his penis deep inside her hot little body. He knew she wouldn't resist him—the chemistry between them was too intense—but he didn't just want her compliance. He wanted…her. All of her. Willing and eager and excited.

The way she'd been that night.

Rance gathered his control, reached for the remote control and flipped through the television channels. He'd just settled on a bull riding competition being broadcast live from Las Vegas when Deanie finally emerged from the bathroom.

"Ready," she breathed, drawing his full attention.

She wore the sundress he'd seen her purchase in the boutique, a pair of high heels that arched her back. Her legs seemed longer, an endless stretch of pale, smooth skin that started at mid-thigh where her dress ended. Her breasts looked full and rounded beneath the strappy top. Her hair hung loose and flowing. Pink lip gloss slicked her full lips.

It was all he could do not to cross the room to her and see if she tasted even half as good as she looked.

She would taste even better. He knew that from the storage closet at the airport and he also knew that once he started kissing her again, he wasn't going to be able to stop.

Which was why Rance intended to let her initiate the next kiss between them. He could do any and everything, from running his hands through her silky hair, to licking every inch of her body. That was just sex. But kissing? That went much deeper and so he wouldn't do it again.

Willing and eager and excited.

"What was so private about a transmission?" he asked as she moved to retrieve her purse.

Her mouth drew into a tight line. "You eavesdropped?"

"You mentioned the transmission before you ran into the bathroom. What's with all the secrecy?"

"I just wanted to give Miss Judy my full attention."

"I wouldn't have bothered you."

"The air conditioner's a little noisy."

"It's barely humming."

She turned on him. "Look, it's my business, okay?" She shook her head. "I mean, it used to be my business. It's not anymore, but Miss Judy had a few questions and so I answered them. Her transmission has a slow leak that I've been patching for the past year. Nothing that requires a new one at this point. But the mechanics at Big Daddy's are trying to tell her that's her only recourse."

"You must be a really good mechanic."

It was as if his words reminded her of something and she shook her head. "I'm sorry. I know you don't want to hear shop talk."

"Why the career change? Why not just quit Big Daddy and go to work over at Merle's?" Merle was Big Daddy's only competition and Rance knew from her reputation under the hood that Merle would have given her a job in a heartbeat.

"Can you see me do that dressed like this?" Deanie shook her head. "I'm tired of being a mechanic, that's all."

"Is it?" His question made her pause. Her gaze caught his and he saw her anguish. She nibbled her bottom lip as if she couldn't decide what to say. Or how much to say.

"I'm a woman," she finally murmured. "But nobody treats me like one. Sure, I've had the occasional boyfriend, but it's never been anything serious. I want serious." Desperation and a fierce sense of longing filled her eyes. "I'm tired of sitting home alone on Friday nights. I want to share my life with someone. I want them to bring me roses and remember my birthday." She blinked, her eyes suddenly bright and Rance's chest tightened. "I know that sounds crazy. I mean, the closest I've come to a dozen roses was the time I mowed over Mrs. Willaby's prize-winning bush that summer I was helping my brother, Cory, cut yards for extra money." She shook her head. "I was always one of the boys. But I'm not now. I'm a woman and I want to feel like one." The moment the words were out, she clamped her mouth shut for a long moment, as if she regretted saying anything. "That sounds crazy, huh?"

He pushed to his feet and stepped toward her while she eyed him. "Aren't you going to say anything?" she finally asked. "What are you thinking?"

"That it's Friday night."

Realization seemed to dawn in her eyes and a grin played at her mouth. "It is Friday, isn't it?"

He nodded. "And you're not sitting home alone." He took her hand in his. "Not this time."

Not ever, a voice whispered.

Because Rance had the gut feeling that Deanie Codge just might be the one thing missing from his life.

9

"THIS PLACE IS BEAUTIFUL," Deanie said as she and Rance approached the entrance to The Falls.

"You haven't seen anything yet." Rance barely resisted the urge to capture her slick, pouty lips in a kiss that would surely have them skipping dinner and going straight to the dessert. "Erica sent us," Rance told the hostess, and recognition dawned.

"You're Rance McGraw."

He winked. "That's me."

"Just a second, Mr. McGraw." She picked up the microphone and pressed the on button. "Erica, please report to the hostess stand."

A few moments later, the bellhop appeared and gave Rance an it's-all-good grin. "Right this way Mr. McGraw. We have your table waiting." She grabbed two menus off the top of the stack and motioned for them to follow.

Rance cupped Deanie's elbow to steady her as she navigated the path in her man-killer shoes. The heat from her body seeped into his fingertips and stirred his hunger even more, and the muscles in his arms bunched and tightened. His groin throbbed.

He was this close to losing it, but the tremble of her body as she took each step reminded him that he had to take things slow. She wasn't nearly the sex goddess she appeared to be, and while Rance meant to seduce her to the point of no return, he had no intention of scaring her off before he could do it.

Breathe, he told himself. *Just hold up and breathe.*

The trouble with that bit of advice was that every draft of air he drank in smelled of sweet vanilla and honey and *her.*

For a split second, the past pulled him back and he remembered the first time he'd really noticed the scent. Deanie had been in the eighth grade and he'd been a junior at Romeo High.

They'd gone to different schools, but they'd still ridden the same bus the long distance home every day. He'd taken to sitting with Sandra Whatshername who'd been the head cheerleader back then and queen of the daring divas—the pretty, popular girls who'd had a thing for sexy clothes, lots of makeup and big hair. It was common knowledge that they'd gone through cans of Aqua Net faster than Mr. Gantry, the local pharmacist, could keep it in stock. In fact, rumor had it that the divas alone were responsible for the beachfront retirement condo he'd purchased down in Fort Lauderdale a few years back.

Deanie had been younger and as far from a daring diva as a girl could get. He'd realized that the day Sandra had been sick and he'd ended up sitting next to Deanie on the bus—she'd saved him a seat as usual.

It had been early September and hotter than Hell on a Saturday night. The bus window had stuck and so he'd reached around Deanie—who'd been sitting next to the window—to help her slide the glass down. Her hair had brushed his jaw— *brushed,* not scratched—and he'd inhaled the sweet scent of Miss Myrtle's homemade honey shampoo. He'd drank in a few deep breaths and the aroma had stayed with him long after he'd climbed off the bus and walked the winding road to the ranch house.

His nostrils flared and the familiar scent filled his head again. For all the changes she'd made, she was obviously still using the homemade stuff that was still bottled and sold at the local pharmacy. His fingers itched to reach out now and feel the long strands spill through his fingers.

But as tempted as he was, he wanted more than

just to be inside of Deanie's sweet body. He wanted inside her head. Her heart.

Now wait a minute. Wait just a damned minute.

The lust eating him up from the inside out had nothing to do with her heart and everything to do with her hot little body accented by the revealing sundress. It wasn't as if Rance wanted to fall in love and settle down. He had places to go and things to see. Christ, he wasn't even sure he believed in the concept. Sure, he'd lusted after women. But love? He'd never loved any woman.

Except maybe this one.

The notion lingered in his head as he guided Deanie through a maze of tables situated here and there around the lush lagoon. Water plunged over a wall of rocks and fed the pool in a steady stream.

Deanie paused at the last table, as if she expected to be seated. But Erica motioned for them to keep following her, around a huge potted palm toward a door cut into the rocks just to the side of the waterfall. An Employees Only sign had been posted. The hostess glanced behind them as if to make sure that no one was looking, pulled a small key from her pocket and unlocked the large dead bolt that barred the entrance.

A few seconds later, she led them through a small tunnel lit by a single overhead bulb. The *whooshing* noise grew louder as they navigated the walkway that opened into a large, cavelike room directly behind the waterfall.

When Erica had told him this was *the* most romantic spot on the island, he'd been skeptical. Hell, it was a *cave.* Naturally, he'd envisioned dark and dank and loud.

He'd been wrong.

The waterfall created a shimmering curtain, accented by colored spotlights on the other side. It was thick enough that the restaurant patrons seemed little more than indistinguishable blurs. The only thing visible was the candlelight that glittered from the center of each table, a reminder of the world that existed just beyond the rushing veil of water. White linen draped the single table that had been set up in the center of the room. Elaborate settings of china and crystal sparkled in the dim light. The plates steamed with fresh vegetables and rice. A pair of matching steaks overflowed a platter surrounded by freshly cut mangoes and pineapples chunks. A bottle of wine chilled nearby in a silver ice bucket.

"The locals used to slip in and out of here on a pretty regular basis," Erica told them. As loud as the waterfall seemed, she didn't have to raise her voice. It echoed off the walls, making the noise seem little more than a steady murmur. "But then Mr. Castellano—he's the owner of Escapades—found out. He had a door built over the opening and now he keeps the entrance padlocked." She smiled and held up the key. "But my boyfriend's sister dates the restaurant manager who's in charge of changing the lightbulbs on the spotlights attached to the rocks. There's no other way to do that except through here."

"This is the only key that I know of, so no one should disturb you." She handed Rance the piece of metal. "Just throw the dead bolt behind me and enjoy."

"Thanks," Rance told the young woman as he left Deanie staring openmouthed at the elaborate table and followed Erica back through the short tunnel.

"No problem, Mr. McGraw. I owe you."

"For an autographed T-shirt?" He shook his head. "I'm the one who owes you. Everything looks great." He moved to retrieve his wallet from his shorts, but she waved him away.

"I don't want your money."

"Then what do you want?"

Hope glimmered in her eyes. "For you to come and watch us ride in the morning, maybe give us a few pointers. You don't know how totally bitchin' it would be to have the USA wakeboard champion give us advice."

"I'll be there."

She grinned and left. Rance threw the dead bolt behind her and turned to head back to Deanie. He found her staring at the curtain of water, her back to him.

"I've never seen anything quite like this."

"I've never seen anything quite like you," he murmured as he came up behind her. "You look really great."

"Funny what a difference a new dress can make. If you'd told me five years ago that I would be standing here, wearing a get-up like this, I would have knocked you on your ass." She paused. "I mean butt."

"Don't tell me, ultra-femme women don't say ass."

"I'm sure they do, but the only ultra-femme female I've ever actually known didn't. And she would have washed my mouth out with soap if she'd have heard me say it." She smiled. "My grandmother was something. I miss her, but I never really realized how much until lately."

"I miss my parents, too." He wasn't sure why he said it, except he felt it at that moment and it seemed only natural that he tell Deanie.

Hell, even when he didn't tell her, she knew.

She knew him. Now, just as she had back then.

"You miss your home, too," she said as if she read his thoughts.

"I don't get over to Austin nearly as much as I used to," he said, referring to the two-story colonial he'd bought near Lake Travis the year before. "I still have boxes stacked in the game room."

"Not that home. Romeo. The Iron Horse." She cast a sideways glance at him. "You miss it."

He didn't say anything for a long moment. He finally shrugged. "Sometimes."

"It's okay. I miss it, too. Not enough to go back, but I still miss it. I didn't realize how much until today when Miss Margie called me. And then Miss Judy. I feel bad leaving them."

"Then don't."

"I have to. I need to get away."

"You mean, you need to run away."

"I'm not running away from anything. I'm going to something. Something much better than what I left behind."

"That's what I always thought, too."

What he'd convinced himself to be the gospel truth. Truthfully, he'd left for a football career because it had been his one and only ticket out of Romeo at a time when he'd been desperate to leave and escape his grandfather's grief. The old man had turned his back on Rance and his brothers and pushed them away from the time Rance's parents had died, until the boys had graduated high school. And then he'd stopped pushing because all three boys had run on their own.

The oldest of the triplets, Josh, had left to get his pilot's license and open a charter service in Arizona. Mason, the middle McGraw, had pursued the rodeo circuit where he'd won title after title before taking his winnings and opening his own ranch management consulting group. And Rance had busted his ass playing a sport he didn't really love because he'd been good at it and he'd been able to pick the college of his choice.

He'd known he would never make it out of Romeo by wrestling steers. While the sport earned some decent prize money, the real cash had been in bull riding. Rance had settled for the next best thing—busting heads out on the football field. It had been hard at first, but eventually he'd stopped missing the steer wrestling all together.

At least that's what he'd told himself.

What he was still telling himself.

He just wasn't so sure he believed it anymore. The rush of adrenaline that came with each competition was less potent and more fleeting. Not to mention, the events were getting more outlandish and over the top. Today alligator wrestling in Australia. Tomorrow? He wouldn't be surprised to find himself surfing the middle of a hurricane or battling a group of crazed women shoppers at a Victoria's Secret Semiannual Sale.

It wasn't the danger that bothered him. It was the craziness of it all. A craziness that just didn't make his heart pound as fiercely as it once had.

Not like it was pounding right now with Deanie standing so close. Feeling so warm. Smelling so sweet.

"Have you ever thought about moving back to Romeo?" She asked him the one question he'd been asking himself since he'd broken his leg.

He'd gone back home on purpose. To remind himself what a dried up place it was and how bored he would be sitting around listening to his great-aunt Lurline and great-uncle Eustess argue about everything from the *Jerry Springer Show* to the perfect temperature to reheat oatmeal.

Bor-ing.

Only it hadn't felt that way. He'd sat on the porch in the evening, the sun setting just on the horizon, the crickets buzzing around him, Eustess and Lurline arguing up a storm just a few feet away, and it had felt familiar. And warm. And right.

Just like now.

"Have you?" she prodded.

He shrugged. "Maybe."

"Not me. I'm never going back."

"To Romeo, or to the old Deanie?" The one who'd lived and breathed in his memories for so long.

"Both." Before he could ask her another question, she turned. "So what is all this for?"

"Aren't you hungry?"

"Well, yes. But I'm not missing the aphrodisiac foods workshop. That isn't until next week."

"This isn't about food. It's about Using Your Environment," he recited the name of the second workshop. "It's about letting everything around you heighten your sexual experience."

Hope lit her eyes. "So we're going to have a sexual experience?" *Finally,* her gaze seemed to add and he couldn't help but smile.

"First we're going to eat." He pulled out a chair and motioned her to sit.

"Just eating?" She eyed him before she sank into the chair.

"And soaking up the atmosphere." He seated himself across from her, reached for the bottle of wine and proceeded to pour them each a glass. "Sex isn't just about the main event. It's about bringing your senses alive. That's what this place is for. It sets the mood for what comes next." He popped a piece of pineapple into his mouth and chewed so slowly that it made her visibly swallow.

"Right now, we're going to enjoy that mood," he went on. He licked his lips and tasted the pineapple. His stomach grumbled for more. For her. "And then," he added, his gaze capturing hers, "we'll be moving on to The Power Of Touching, and we'll be enjoying each other."

"I DON'T KNOW ABOUT THIS," Deanie said an hour later as Rance used a fresh linen napkin to fashion a blindfold over her eyes.

"Number three is all about touching. You don't need to see a thing. Just feel." His hands dropped to her shoulders. His fingertips played down her arms and a shiver worked its way up her spine.

The semi darkness made the hot play of his hands that much more intense as they traveled back up her arms, down her shoulder blades to the plunging back of her sundress. He unfastened the buttons, peeled the dress down her shoulders, and then she felt the soft cotton of his T-shirt against her bare back. His hands slid around her ribs and came up to cup her trembling breasts. She sagged against him and her head fell back onto his shoulder.

He caught her nipples between his fingers and rolled the sensitive nubs until a gasp parted her lips. Then he moved on, *down,* and smoothed his palm down her belly to where her dress had caught at her hips. Hooking his fingers beneath the material, he worked it over her bottom and pushed it down the length of her legs until she stepped free.

"You took my advice," he finally murmured. His voice came from in front of her this time.

He didn't pull her to him the way she expected. The way she'd been anticipating over the past hour as they'd eaten and talked and eyed each other across the small table. The cavelike room was massive, but it seemed cozy and intimate with Rance filling up her line of vision and watching her every movement. By the time the meal had ended, she'd been ready to jump him.

Thankfully, he'd grabbed the linen napkin and initiated the next workshop.

The heat of his body drew her and she knew he was right in front of her. Close. But not close enough.

Her breath caught when she felt a fingertip at her belly button. The rough pad slid south in a slow, tor-turous trek that caught the air in her lungs and held it there until he reached the small triangle of curls between her legs. "You left off the panties."

"No... I mean, yes. But not on purpose. I forgot

them when I grabbed my stuff and went into the bathroom. We left so fast after that that I didn't have a chance to put them on."

He didn't say anything for a long moment. Instead, the sound of her own heart thundered in her ears.

"How did it feel without them?" he finally asked.

"Weird." The word was little more than a sigh as he slid one finger down and parted her slick folds. "At, um, first."

"And after that?"

"Exciting." She felt the rush of wetness between her legs as he stroked her. She licked her lips and wondered how much she should tell him. But then he grazed her clitoris and the words tumbled out on a gasp. "I could feel the dress against my bare bottom." She drew a breath and licked her lips. "With each step. Pulling this way and pushing that way."

"Rubbing you?" While he played her with one hand, the other slid around to stroke her butt cheek. "Here?" She nodded. "And what about here?" He moved his finger back and forth in her slick folds. "What did it feel like?"

"It felt…sexy. I felt sexy." The admission was out before she could stop it. Oddly enough, she didn't feel any regret. It was the blindfold, she told herself. It leant a sense of anonymity to the situation. He didn't see her and she didn't see him, and so there was no embarrassment.

"You *are* sexy, Deanie. With or without panties."

Before the comment could sink in, he pulled away. She heard the clink of dishes, the rustle of linen and then he caught her hands. She felt the hard edge of the table press into her bottom. Hard, hot hands urged her down until she was totally stretched out.

His hands lingered at her breasts, his palms rubbing the tips in a circular motion that made them swell and throb. He pulled away and she felt the warm night air caress her body for several breathless moments before something cool and juicy touched one ripe peak. Her nostrils flared and the scent of pineapple filled her head and saturated her senses.

She felt a dribble of sticky sweetness glide down her breast a split second before Rance caught the wetness with the hot flick of his tongue.

"You taste sweet," he murmured.

"I thought this workshop focused on touch."

"It does, but there's nothing wrong with a little taste now and then."

He pressed the piece of pineapple against her bottom lip and she opened her mouth. She expected him to slide the piece of lush fruit past her lips. Instead, his breath brushed her mouth a heartbeat before he caught her bottom lip between his teeth and suckled.

She felt a pull in her nipples and a steady throb started between her legs.

"I thought I was getting the taste?" she breathed, marveling at how sexy her voice sounded. How natural.

"That doesn't come until Taste 101. Now, the only thing you need to worry about is feeling. Leave the tasting to me."

He touched the pineapple chunk to her lips again before sliding it down her neck. Her breasts tingled and tightened in anticipation of where he would go next. He circled each nipple with the succulent fruit before moving lower. She felt the cool wetness glide down her stomach, over the top of one thigh, the inside of her knee before moving north again along her inner thigh. The fruit barely grazed her hot folds before finding the inside of her other thigh and starting the same trek down.

She braced herself to feel the soft, lush wetness against her sex, but when it came this time, there was no fleeting zap of electricity. Instead, Rance traced her hot slit up and down with the chunk of pineapple before parting her and nudging the fruit into her opening. Electricity sizzled across her nerve endings and her body went taut at the sudden pressure between her legs.

He nudged the fruit just a fraction more into her and then… Nothing.

He'd pulled away and the only sound was that of her heart pounding in her ears.

"Christ, you're beautiful," he murmured, the words so raw and husky that she almost didn't hear them. But with her vision gone, her other senses had, indeed, heightened. "So damned beautiful."

A strange warmth unfolded in her chest and she had the sudden urge to reach for him, to kiss him, to *love* him.

Just as the disturbing thought struck, he captured her mouth in a deep, wet kiss and her brain scrambled. His tongue pushed inside to stroke and coax for a long moment that left her breathless and panting when he finally dragged his mouth away and followed the path he'd taken with the pineapple.

He licked and nibbled his way down her neck, between her breasts. His tongue flicked out and lapped at one nipple before drawing it deep into his mouth. He suckled her, drawing hard on the sensitive tip for a long moment before sliding his lips over to deliver the same torture to her other breast.

The darkness didn't seem so dark anymore. Tiny

pinpoints of light danced in front of her. Her breaths came short and shallow. Her knees trembled and her tummy tingled and her body clenched around the pineapple he'd wedged inside of her.

Her hands came up and threaded in his soft, silky hair as his mouth proceeded downward again. He lapped at her belly button before following the same path he'd taken with the pineapple. Down one leg to her knee, back up the inside of her thigh. Down the other leg and back up and… *Yes!*

His lips grazed her clitoris and desire jolted through her. Her back arched and she would have come up off the table if he hadn't slid his hands beneath her buttocks and pulled her to the edge. She heard the heavy thud as he dropped to his knees and then his mouth was on her again. His tongue parted her folds and he lapped at the fruit nestled inside the opening of her slick passage. And then he sucked. At the same time, her body tightened around the lush fruit.

His mouth played tug-of-war with her for several pulse-pounding moments. She felt the pressure and gasped as he sucked harder and longer.

The pinpoints of light danced and spun until they all seemed to collide into one brilliant flash. Rance drew on her so hard and so perfectly that the pineapple slid into his mouth just as every muscle in her body went rigid. Her climax hit her hard and fast and she exploded with a pleasure so intense that it frightened her.

Or maybe it was the look in Rance's eyes when he whipped off the blindfold and stared at her, into her, that scared the bejeesus out of her. While she trembled and shook with the force of *the* best orgasm of her entire life, raw hunger brightened his gaze, along with a fierce, possessive light she'd never seen before.

As if he'd just realized that she was his and he never meant to let her go.

Not tomorrow.

Not ever.

Not likely.

The entire time they'd been growing up, he'd never once considered that she might be The One. He certainly wasn't going to reconsider in a few hours. Deanie knew his sudden attraction had nothing to do with newly discovered feelings and everything to do with her makeover.

He wanted her, all right, but not in a forever kind of way. And even if he did—we're talking a big *if*—it wasn't really Deanie, herself, that drew him. It was the sexy, ultra-femme version she was trying her damndest to be.

She tamped down her disappointment. Sex, she

reminded herself. Keep it short—sixteen hours left and counting—and keep it simple. No falling in love again.

The trouble was, Deanie was starting to realize that she'd never fallen out of love in the first place. And the more time she spent with him, the harder it was to keep from peeling off her clothes and making the same offer—the same mistake—all over again.

Hard, but not impossible.

Not yet.

10

HE WASN'T GOING TO TOUCH HER.

Rance made that vow to himself as he walked Deanie back to her hotel room after dinner at The Falls. She was so close, keeping time beside him, a strange look on her face.

As if she couldn't quite believe what had just happened.

He didn't blame her. His heart pounded and his chest hitched and it was all he could do to make his feet keep moving forward. Her ripe sweet taste lingered on his tongue and her musky scent filled his nostrils. The image of her naked and spread out on the table before him rooted in his mind. He could still feel her sex quivering against his lips. Her cries echoed in his head and made his blood pump faster and more furious through his body.

But it wasn't the memory that shook his control and made him hard-pressed to keep his distance. Or hard, period. It was the desire for more. Hunger gnawed at his gut. He wanted to be inside of her and feel her hot, sweet body contract around his. He wanted to stare deep into her eyes and see the desire reflected in her gaze.

That meant no blindfolds to hide behind. No workshops to excuse the heat that burned between them. Nothing but the two of them kissing and touching and *loving*.

There was that word again, poking and prodding and making him think as he eyed Deanie who stood next to him on the elevator.

She nibbled on her bottom lip, her cheeks still flushed. Her eyes shone bright and blue with desire and desperation whenever she happened to glance at him. Which, he noted, was when she thought he wasn't looking at her.

He looked at her now, openly studying her as he contemplated the notion of loving Deanie Codge. Could he really have fallen for her? Hard and fast and past the point of no return? *Hell, no.* That's what reason told him. At the same time, he wanted her too much to explain away his feelings as lust. He wanted her to want him too much.

He needed it.

It's your ego, buddy. Your pride.

That's what he'd told himself in the beginning. But truthfully, he couldn't give a shit about his pride now. Christ, he was this close to pushing her up against the elevator and sliding fast and deep and sure inside of her, to hell with her admitting that she still had a crush on him.

He would have done just that if he hadn't glimpsed the longing that flashed in her gaze every now and then, along with regret.

She was scared of him, plain and simple.

Not physically, but emotionally.

That's why she'd let him touch her earlier by the pool. Because her back had been to him and she hadn't had to look at him, to see her emotions reflected in his gaze. When they had been face-to-face and he'd been staring at her, into her, she'd been spooked, and so she'd tossed him into the water. Tonight, she'd had the blindfold to hide behind.

She wasn't afraid of the explosive chemistry between them. Rather, she was scared of what she felt for him. The thing was, the chemistry was explosive *because* of what she felt. Because the feelings ran deeper than lust.

The elevator doors slid open and they stepped out onto her floor. Her arm brushed his as she moved past. Desire bolted through him and his balls tightened. Every muscle in his body flexed. His spine stiffened. He longed to reach out, pull her into his arms and kiss her until all the barriers crumbled and there was no denying what she felt. Not for his pride's sake, mind you—he couldn't give a shit if she admitted her feelings to him. Rather, he wanted her to admit them to herself.

Because, for the first time in his life, Rance wanted more from a woman than sex. He wanted her heart.

He wanted Deanie's.

And?

And so he wasn't going to touch her again. Or push. Or give her any reason to back away from him.

The next move was hers.

If only he would touch her again.

The desperate thought played through Deanie's head as she tried to slide the key card into the slot. But Rance stood so close behind her, his body so hard and hot and *there,* that she had trouble thinking, much less functioning. The card went in, but the green light refused to come on.

Pulling the blasted piece of plastic free, she tried to gather her determination. Her hands trembled as she shoved the key into the opening a second time.

"Whatever happened to regular old keys?" she grumbled when the red light continued to shine.

"These are safer," Rance said. His hand came

up to steady hers and guide the card toward the slot. The plastic went in and slid out, and the traitorous green light blinked. He reached around her and opened the door.

But where he'd lingered with the contact earlier that day, he didn't press his lips to her temple or brush his mouth against her ear, or do anything even remotely suggestive.

Because he isn't half as turned on as you are.

A wave of disappointment rolled through her. Her stomach hollowed out as she stepped into her hotel room and Rance made no move to follow.

She turned, one trembling hand on the doorknob. "Thanks for walking me back." *And giving me the most amazing orgasm of my life.*

Her cheeks flamed at the memory. She licked her lips and he followed the action with his gaze. His eyes darkened to rich, golden pools so deep she could only imagine how far she would have to go to reach the bottom.

She knew then that while she might be close to losing control and forgetting all about her self-made promise, Rance was just as close.

Could she push him over the edge? She had to, otherwise she would be begging him and *that* wasn't going to happen.

"I'll see you later." He started to turn.

"Wait," she blurted. She leaned against the doorjamb and tried for a sexy, come-and-get-me pose. "I, um, really enjoyed dinner." She went for a breathless, excited voice, but the words sounded more like she had a bad case of laryngitis. She cleared her throat. "I don't think I've ever been any place quite that incredible."

He raked a hand through his hair and glanced down the hallway as if sizing up his chances for a quick escape. "The place was pretty incredible, all right." Another glance and Deanie grew even more determined.

"You were pretty incredible, yourself." The statement earned his full attention. "I definitely think I'm learning a lot." She drew a deep breath, letting the air fill her lungs and push her breasts up and out. The bodice of her dress tightened, outlining her ripe nipples.

Rance's attention, however, didn't leave her face. Instead, his gaze held hers, trying to understand her sudden boldness.

She ignored the fear that niggled at her gut. It wasn't like she was tossing her pride out in favor of jumping his bones. She was merely using her newfound feminine wiles to tempt *him* into jumping *her* bones.

"So what's next?" she asked him. "I'm free of my

inhibitions. I know all about using my environment. And I'm well aware of the power of touching."

"We do erogenous zones next." His gaze dropped then, drinking in the display her nipples made as they pressed greedily beneath the dress.

"You mean here?" Deanie reached up and touched one achingly ripe peak. She traced the point it made beneath the fabric. Her breath caught and her heart seemed to stop. She'd done her fair share of masturbating over the years, and she'd stroked herself. But never with anyone watching her. Or wanting her as much as he did.

A muscle twitched in his jaw and a golden light fired in the center of his pupils.

She guided her fingertip to the other aching breast and touched the peak. "And here?"

"Yeah." His voice was deep and husky and he looked ready to snatch her hand away and touch her himself.

If only.

"What about here?" Her hand dropped to—

He caught her fingers midair. Before she could blink, he pulled her flush against him. His lips captured hers, his tongue plunged deep, stroking and coaxing until her surprise fled and she joined him. Her tongue tangled and delved and tasted, and she gave as good as she got.

Her toes curled, her nerves came alive, and a sizzling heat swept through her, starting where his lips touched hers and spreading outward in a search and destroy mission and she all but melted in his arms.

Her hands snaked around his neck, pulling him closer. She leaned into him and fit her hips to his. His cock pressed rock-hard against her sex. Her aching breasts pushed against the soft material of her sundress, desperate to get free and feel the heat of the man in her arms.

And he burned so hot.

His skin seemed to fire to life beneath her touch.

Everywhere she stroked, caressed, she felt a prickling sensation, his body alive and humming. The sensation stirred her nerves and set them to spinning until she felt as charged, as vibrant as the man touching her.

He splayed one hand at the base of her spine, pressing her closer while his other bunched the hem of her sundress until the rough pads of his fingers grazed her thigh. He slid his hand around to cup her bottom and knead the soft flesh. He kissed and fondled her until she knew beyond a doubt that he did, indeed, want her as much as she wanted him.

That he meant to have her.

Finally.

Thankfully.

The knowledge sang through her and she broke the kiss long enough to slide her mouth down his chin, his neck, to his pulse beat. She licked the spot before moving down, through a forest of silky hair. She suckled a brown male nipple and explored the rippled expanse of his abdomen. He groaned long and low and deep and she had the sudden urge to drop to her knees in front of him and love him with her mouth the way he'd loved her. He was all hard muscle and hot skin and she wanted him so much.

More than she wanted her next breath.

The realization jerked Deanie back to reality just as her fingers grazed the bulge beneath his shorts. She froze and his hand covered hers. She expected him to urge her on. She wanted him to, to take the decision away from her. The responsibility. The regret.

He let his hand fall away from hers and he simply stared at her for several heart pounding moments. Fierce, golden eyes drilled into hers as he waited for her to make her choice, to act on it.

She wanted to.

More than she wanted her next breath.

"It's getting really late," she blurted. Her hand

fell away and she curled her fingers as she stepped back, despite her body, that urged her the other way. Back into his arms.

Her cell phone rang from the nightstand where she'd left it, the sound barely pushing past the thunder of her own heart. The pain of crying herself to sleep every night after he'd left and the fear that she would never, ever feel so strongly for someone again swirled together and fought against the desire that burned deep inside.

Her cell phone continued to ring.

"You should really go," she told him.

"If that's what you want." His gaze held hers and he reached out, his hand touching her cheek. "Is that what you want, Deanie? What you *really* want?"

"Yes." At that moment, it *was* what she really wanted. She needed him to leave before she lost her control and threw herself into his arms.

Before she lost herself.

"Okay." But he didn't sound the least bit okay. He sounded angry and disappointed and, oddly enough, hurt.

He leaned down, gave her a rough kiss, and then he walked away and left Deanie with her pride still intact.

The damnable thing was, she didn't feel half as relieved as she should have.

Instead, she felt alone. Lonely.

She didn't give herself a chance to dwell on the notion. She closed the door and went to retrieve her cell phone which had stopped ringing only to start again, as if the person on the other end hadn't been the least bit content to leave a message.

Deanie glanced at the caller ID and worry, along with a hefty dose of surprise, rushed through her.

"Miss Eloise?"

"Deanie? Is that you, honey?"

"Yes, ma'am."

"Praise be to Jesus! Why, I just knew you'd been snatched up by one of those cannibals and turned into someone's lunch."

"Excuse me?"

"Despite all the fancy pants stuff the world is into, there are still primitive tribes in existence. Why, I saw this group called the Jiminy Crickets, or something like that, who actually baste and barbecue any stranger who disturbs their sacred hunting ground. Speaking of hunting, I wished you would have taken old Junior, here." Junior was Eloise's late husband's prizewinning duck dog. He'd turned fifteen last year and the only title he'd won recently was for oldest canine in the county. "I would feel so much better knowing you were protected." A loud bark sounded in the background and Miss Eloise paused to baby talk the ancient animal. "Then again," she finally continued, "if they'll eat a dear, sweet girl like you, they would probably go nuts for my Junior. Have you got Mace?"

"They don't allow Mace on the airplane."

"What about a can of Aqua Net? I was watching Court TV the other day and they had a case where this woman used a can of the stuff on a would-be rapist and it damn near blinded him. The key is to aim right for the pupil."

"I'm fine, Miss Eloise."

"At least that's true for one of us."

"What's wrong?"

"Harwin says Betty Lou needs new shocks. An entire set."

Betty Lou was Miss Eloise's 1972 Cadillac. The car was older than Deanie herself, but in mint condition. Eloise's late husband had loved the automobile almost as much as he'd loved Miss Eloise herself. At least that had been the gossip down at the Fat Cow Diner when he'd opted to wash and wax the car rather than take Miss Eloise out for their fiftieth anniversary. Miss Eloise hadn't been too fond of Betty Lou after that. But then her husband had died and the car had been all she'd had left of him, and so the two females had warmed up to each other.

"I just put a new set of shocks on her last year," Deanie said.

"I told Harwin that, but he said you didn't do it right." She paused. "And he also said that I might have hit too many potholes."

"Did you hit a lot?"

"One, give or take a few."

"How few?"

"Maybe six or seven."

"Miss Eloise, you have to be careful. The car rides low. You'll bottom out."

"I know that, honey. That's why I try my best to go around them, but they always seem to snag that front left tire."

"Then Harwin should try changing the front left connecting shocks first before replacing them all. An entire new set is going to cost you—"

"—my teeth money," the old woman retorted. "I've been saving all year for a new set of dentures."

"Shocks don't cost quite that much, Miss Eloise."

"They do if they're being accompanied by a new muffler."

"What's wrong with your muffler?"

"It got jarred loose when I hit the pothole over on Main and Divine. The one in front of the dry cleaners."

"There's no pothole there."

"There is now on account of Wilda Jean was getting a new press iron and the delivery people dropped it and made a crack in the asphalt. And then I came along and, well, you know how heavy Betty Lou is. So now there's a pothole and I won't be able to get my teeth in time for the Easter Jubilee down at the Bingo Hall. They serve the best brown sugar ham and now I won't be able to have any and—"

"What about a payment plan?" It was Deanie's turn to interrupt. "Just tell Harwin to sign you up for one of Big Daddy's installment options. That way you can still get your shocks and your dentures."

"There are no more installment plans. Harwin did away with them and Big Daddy's going along with it."

"You're kidding?"

Miss Eloise sniffled. "We're talking the brown sugar ham with the glazed pineapple rings on top and the little maraschino cherries."

"You're not kidding." Miss Eloise had two passions in life—watching television and eating—and she didn't joke about either. "I'm sorry, Miss Eloise."

"Now, now, I know it's not your fault. It's not like you can just throw your life away because me and the girls down at the seniors' center need you. You're young. You've got your entire life ahead of you. You shouldn't be burdened by a bunch of old women. Why, we can fend for ourselves just fine. Don't you even worry about us. It's not like I can't gum a few pieces of ham if I set my mind to it. I'll still get all the flavor. Don't you even worry about it."

Okay, so Miss Eloise had three passions in life—watching television, eating and laying major guilt trips.

"I'll call and talk to Big Daddy for you. Maybe he'll make an exception."

"No, no, honey. Why, I would never dream of being such a bother. I just needed to vent. When you get old, there aren't as many people around when you need to talk."

"I'd like to try to help."

"Don't you fret over me. You just go on about your business. This is your time to be young, honey. To enjoy yourself, even if it is a long ways away from those of us who love you dearly."

The old woman was right.

Deanie came to that conclusion a half hour after she'd said goodbye to Miss Eloise. She'd taken a cold shower, pulled on her soft cotton "comfort" T-shirt and sweats, and stretched out on the bed. This *was* her time to be young and she *should* be enjoying it.

Instead, she was channel surfing and eating a bag of Oreos she'd purchased from the minibar.

She glanced at the remote in one hand and the cookie in the other. It was every Friday night she'd ever spent all over again. Granted, she'd actually had a date earlier, and an orgasm, but now she was right back to acting like the old Deanie, despite the fact that Rance still wanted her and she still wanted him.

Want.

It didn't have to go beyond that if she didn't let it. If she cut herself off emotionally from the sex and kept her feelings locked up tight.

Then she could enjoy herself for the next thirteen hours. Couldn't she?

She could.

She would.

She was tired of fantasizing. She wanted the real thing. The real man. Just for a little while. Deep down, she knew no matter where she went, or how hard she searched, or how many low cut dresses she wore, she would never meet another man like Rance McGraw.

He was a one-of-a-kind.

Her first love.

Her last.

She ignored the thought and threw her legs over

the side of the bed. This wasn't about love. It was all about sex. About *having* sex.

Deanie peeled off her clothes, pulled on her sundress—minus the undies again—and reached for her shoes. She glanced at the clock and entertained a rush of anxiety that quickly fed her determination.

Stashing her key card in her one and only pocket, she left the hotel room and went in search of Rance.

IT TOOK DEANIE nearly an hour before she finally found him on a deserted stretch of beach far enough from the resort that she was actually out of breath by the time she reached him. She'd walked the entire resort before she'd seen the blonde who'd shown them to the waterfall room at The Falls. The girl had pointed her in the right direction. Deanie had been skeptical as she'd passed the guest bungalows and traded the lights of the resort for a full moon and a star-dusted sky. But then she'd spotted him sitting on the beach.

He wore only his cowboy hat and his board shorts. His chest was bare, his shoulders broad. His shirt lay in a heap next to his flip-flops. Muscles rippled as he tossed a sea shell into the retreating surf.

Music drifted from the far distance, but otherwise, the only sound was the lull of the waves against the beach and the pounding of Deanie's heart.

She braced herself against any lingering doubts, held tight to her desire and stepped in front of him.

"I've been looking for you everywhere. What are you doing out here?"

He tipped the brim of his hat back and glanced up at her, his gaze dark and glittering in the moonlight. "I needed some fresh air." He stared past her and pitched another shell. "What about you? Can't sleep?"

"Actually—" She swallowed and gathered the courage that had brought her this far. "—I'm too busy thinking to sleep." Her gaze caught and held his. "I can't stop thinking about you." She stepped toward him. "Us." She dropped to her knees. "This." She leaned over and kissed him long and slow and deep, leaving no doubt how much she wanted him.

He returned her kiss, but he made no move to reach out. She leaned back just enough to murmur "I want you, Rance," and then she took his lips in another deep, purposeful kiss.

She waited to feel his hands at her waist, pulling her to him, but he didn't touch her. He wouldn't. He wanted her to want him, to initiate the contact between them.

He wanted her to make the same offer she'd made all those years ago.

The one he'd turned down cold.

He felt anything but cold now. Her palms rested against his bare shoulders, his skin blazing hot beneath her touch, his muscles bunched tight with sexual tension as he waited to see what she would do next.

She had no intention of disappointing him.

Or herself.

Deanie fought against one last wave of fear. Then she straddled him.

11

RANCE BLINKED, but Deanie didn't fade and disappear the way she did in his fantasies.

Because this wasn't a fantasy.

She was real. Warm. *Here.*

She sat astride him, her skin pale and silky in the moonlight. She shimmied her body and hiked her dress to her waist to give her legs some breathing room. With the material out of her way, she spread wider and settled more fully over him. Her bare sex rested atop his cock that throbbed beneath his shorts. She gripped his shoulders, stared deep into his eyes and rubbed herself against him.

She flung her head back and went wild for the next few moments and it was all he could do not to touch her smooth thighs or knead her sweet, round ass or slide his fingers into her wet heat.

But Rance had been waiting for this moment since that night on the river bank. He'd dreamed of it. He wasn't about to hurry things up. He balled his hands into fists against the sand, braced himself and let her work herself up.

"You feel so good." She hesitated then and her gaze met his. It was all he could do not to take her in his arms and chase away the doubt. "Do you like it, too?"

"Baby, you have no idea." His words reassured her and she smiled, a brilliant slash of white in the moonlit darkness. His chest hitched and his breath caught. "You're so beautiful, Deanie."

"So are you," she murmured, her smile fading into something more primitive and determined.

She kept riding him, rubbing herself up and down, creating a delicious friction before she finally leaned back and reached for the waistband of his shorts. He was already so hard that the zipper caught and refused to budge until his hand closed over hers.

He lifted his pelvis and together they slid his zipper the rest of the way down. He pushed his shorts down, pushing his underwear along with it, until his erection sprang thick and heavy toward her. Her fingertip was hot and arousing as she traced a throbbing vein up his rock-hard length, until she reached the silky-smooth head.

Deanie had seen a few male members in her time, but none of them had been near as impressive as Rance. Bold and beautiful, his penis jutted tall, throbbing beneath her tentative touch. She circled the engorged purple head and he sucked in a breath. The sound fed her confidence and she wrapped her hand around him. Heat scorched her fingertips and he arched into her grasp. His fingers curled into the sand. But he didn't touch her.

Not yet.

Her gaze trailed up over a ridged abdomen, a broad chest sprinkled with dark, silky hair, a corded neck, to the chiseled perfection of his face partially hidden in the shadow of his cowboy hat.

She took his hat off, set it aside and stared deep into his whiskey-colored eyes. There was no mistaking the raw, aching need that gripped him. And the uncertainty. And the regret.

"I'm sorry I left that night. I never meant to hurt you."

"You did the right thing." Even as the words slid from her lips, she couldn't quite believe she'd said them. Even more, she felt them. Deep in her heart. Beneath the pain and hurt. "I didn't think so at the time, but I know now why you did it."

"If I had touched you, kissed you, taken you, I wouldn't have been able to leave, and I had to. I couldn't stay. My granddad didn't want me, and I didn't want to. It hurt too much being around him." As much as Rance had reminded his grandfather of the son he'd lost, the old man had reminded Rance of the father he'd lost.

"I know you had to go." She felt the tears burn the backs of her eyes and she blinked against them. "But back then, I didn't want to think about not seeing you every day. I was young and stupid and I offered myself to you for the wrong reason." Not that she hadn't loved him. She had. But she hadn't stripped naked because she'd been eager to take the next step into womanhood. She'd done it out of fear. It had been her last ditch effort to keep him in her life. "I did it because I wanted you to stay."

His gaze grew brighter, hotter. "And now?"

"Now I just want you."

Before she could draw another breath, his mouth covered hers and his tongue thrust between her parted lips. The kiss seemed to go on forever and when he finally pulled away, Deanie couldn't seem to catch her breath.

She fought for air while he reached down into the pocket of his shorts and retrieved a foil packet. A few seconds later, he slid the condom onto his erection, gripped her waist and pulled her closer.

He pressed his hard sex between her legs. The plump head pushed into her just a fraction until she felt her body pulse around his thick shaft. A shiver ripped through her and she slid her hands around his neck and threaded her fingers into his hair. Her nipples tightened, pressing against the thin material of her dress and her thighs trembled.

He kissed her slowly, deeply, before he finally drew away. His heated gaze held hers as he lifted his hips again, pushing into her a fraction more. But it wasn't enough. There was still too much between them.

She braced her hands against his chest and climbed to her feet. She backed up just a few steps and reached for the edge of her dress. Bunching the hem, she pulled it up and over her head. Her nipples hardened against the sudden breeze blowing in off the water and she trembled.

Her breath caught and her heart stopped as a memory rushed at her and for the next few seconds, it was that one night all over again. She heard the ripple of the river behind her and the buzz of crickets. She felt the soft grass beneath her bare feet, the whisper of a breeze against her skin, and the nerve-racking sense of expectancy in the pit of her stomach as she'd waited for his reaction.

His rejection.

Rance's gaze swept the length of her. Fire flared in his eyes, chasing away the sudden chill of self-consciousness that suddenly gripped her. There was no mistaking the emotion in his gaze as it met

hers—a mixture of open hunger and fierce posses-
siveness that told her he wouldn't dream of
walking away from her this time.

Or ever again.

She forced aside the ridiculous notion. She
wasn't silly enough to believe there could be a
happily ever after with Rance. They were even
more different now than they'd been way back
when. They had different lives. Different futures.

No, this wasn't about tomorrow.

It was about right now.

She watched as he stood and shed his shorts completely. He spread his discarded clothes on the sand
before settling back down and motioning for her.

"Come here," he murmured, his voice raw and
husky and stirring.

Anticipation rippled along her spine and every
nerve in her body tingled. She straddled him again,
her knees and calves cushioned now by the soft
cotton of his T-shirt.

She slid the swollen bud of her clitoris against his
engorged penis until she reached the head. She
rubbed from side to side feeling him pulse against
her most tender spot. She gasped when his teeth
caught one nipple and he closed his lips over the sensitive peak. He drew her deep into his mouth and
sucked so hard that she felt the tug between her legs.

She moved a fraction higher and pressed the wet opening of her body over the head of his erection. His hold on her nipple broke as a ragged gasp escaped his lips. She pushed down slightly, letting him stretch her, fill her just enough to make her insides tighten and then she withdrew.

He bucked beneath her and she did it again, pushing down just enough to make her body crave more before pulling back and gasping for air. His hands slid down her back and his large fingers pressed into her bottom as if to pull her back down. But he didn't. While he was now an active participant, this was still her ride and he obviously intended to let her set the pace.

She kissed him then, sucking at his tongue the way her body sucked at the head of his erection.

Over and over.

His muscles bunched tight beneath her fingertips, his body hard and stiff beneath her, until she knew he couldn't take any more.

With a shudder, she slid down over him until she felt the base of his shaft fully against her. His pubic hair teased the sensitive lips of her vagina. He pulsed inside her for a long, heart-stopping moment before he gripped her bottom with both hands and his hips lifted.

He slid deeper. The sensation of being stretched

and filled by the raw strength of him stalled the air in her lungs for several heart-pounding moments.

The pressure between her legs was sharp and sweet. But not half as sharp and sweet as the sudden tightening in her chest when he looked at her, his gaze so fierce and possessive, as if he never meant to let her go.

As if.

Deanie dismissed the thought and fixed her attention on the desire coiling tight in her body. She rocked her hips, riding him with an intensity that made her heart pound and her body throb.

She held his gaze with each movement, determined to brand his every expression into her memory. Until sensation gripped her, so wild and tantalizing, that her breath stalled and her heart all but stopped beating. She couldn't help herself. While she wanted to watch, the only thing she seemed capable of in that next instant was feeling. Her eyes closed and her head fell back.

He held her tight as she pushed down around him. Her body released a warm, sucking rush of moisture. He groaned then, his hands digging into her bottom as he bucked beneath her. His eyes blazed a feverish gold. The muscles in his neck tightened as he surged one last and final time, burying himself deep as he exploded.

She collapsed against him, her head in the curve of his shoulder as she tried to catch her breath. His arms tightened around her and he simply held her then, stroking her back and her bottom as her heart slowly returned to normal.

Oddly enough, it was those stroking, soothing moments afterward that stood out in her mind long after Rance had helped her to her feet and into her clothes, and led her back to his hotel room. While her orgasm had been earth-shattering, what had followed had been life-changing.

Because Deanie had never felt as beautiful, as cherished, as *loved* as she had when Rance had cradled her on the moonlit beach and the water had whispered behind them.

She grasped the feeling close and refused to acknowledge the small voice in her head that told her she would never, ever feel that way with any other man.

It wasn't about the future. It was about making the most of the next few hours and storing enough memories to last her for the rest of her life.

A life without Rance McGraw.

RANCE HAD BARELY OPENED the door of his hotel room when Deanie backed him up against the nearest wall, dropped to her knees and reached for his shorts. The door rocked shut and the room plunged back into darkness. The only light came from the French doors that opened out onto a large balcony filled with potted palms.

Moonlight fell across her face as she stared up at him, but it wasn't enough. He wanted to see every expression, every reaction, every thought.

Groping to his left, he found the light switch. The lamp on the nightstand turned on. His gaze snagged on the phone that sat next to it. The message light blinked and he felt a twinge of guilt. He knew it was Shank with a reminder about tomorrow. The man had already left two others on Rance's cell phone and there were sure to be many more because Rance had yet to call him back and reassure him that he would be on his way to the Land Down Under by noon the following day.

He would, he reminded himself. It wasn't as if he could just walk away.

Even if he suddenly wanted to.

He vowed to call Shank first thing in the morning, hit the erase button to kill the blinking light and turned his attention back to Deanie.

The pale yellow glow pushed back the shadows and illuminated her face. Her cheeks flushed a bright pink and her lips trembled. Her blue eyes glittered with desire as she reached for him again. He didn't stop her this time. The air stalled in his lungs as he waited. Watched.

She slid the button free and worked the zipper down.

His erection sprang hot and greedy toward her. A drop of pearly liquid beaded on the ripe purple head and she reached out. She caught his essence and spread it in one sensual stroke of her fingertip from tip to root. A growl vibrated from deep in his chest.

She wrapped her hand around him and he arched into her touch, his iron-hard sex dark and forbidden against her slender, pale fingers. She smiled up at him before she leaned forward. Her expression faded into one of serious intent as she lapped at him with her tongue, once, twice, before taking him into her mouth.

Her hair brushed against his belly. The soft, sweet-smelling strands teased his skin and stoked the fire that burned inside of him. Rance caught her long, silky hair and pulled the dark curtain away from her face. He watched as she suckled and licked and caused a pleasure so fierce he didn't think he could stand it.

He did.

He grew harder, hotter, heavier, and she relished her effect on him. He saw it in the confident way she held him and the purposeful slide of her mouth up and down and… *Christ, she felt good.*

She took all of him, relished him, until he came so close to exploding…

"No!" He gasped and jerked back, catching himself just in time. He drew a shaky breath that did nothing to calm his thundering heart and everything to stir his hunger that much more. The scent of her— so potent and sweet and sexy—filled his nostrils, stirred his nerves and shook his already tenuous control. "Not like this." His cock throbbed, the feeling just this side of painful, and his balls ached, but he drew on what little control he had left. He grasped her shoulders and set her away from him.

She stared up, her eyes hot and luminous, mirroring the desperation he felt inside. But there was something else—the insecurity she tried so hard to hide with her makeup and her new clothes and her high heels.

It was still there because she was still there.

Still the same Deanie.

Still hopelessly and desperately in love with him.

The thought struck and his heart missed its next beat.

Yeah, right, buddy. She's all grown up now. She's out of here tomorrow and there isn't a damned thing you can do about it.

Like hell. He could change her mind if he wanted to.

If.

But Rance had his own commitments. He couldn't just walk away.

He knew that, but it didn't stop him from picking her up and striding to the large bathroom. He wanted to touch every inch of her luscious little body in ways no man ever had or ever would.

Because Deanie Codge was his.

At least for tonight.

He set her on her feet and turned on the water. Hot steam rose in the marble and glass enclosure. But the heat didn't come close to touching his rapidly soaring body temperature.

"I'm already wet," she told him with a smile. "You don't have to go to this much trouble."

"This isn't about trouble, darlin'. It's about erogenous zones." He grinned. "We still have one workshop left. Now," he said as he reached around for the straps of her sundress, "the female body has lots of hot spots."

"And you know this because of your vast experience, right?"

"That, and I read the course description posted on the internet. They give several examples." He knew she'd probably read the same, but she played along.

She arched one perfectly-shaped eyebrow. "Such as?"

"Your neck for starters." He unfastened the halterlike top and let the straps fall away. The material fell to her waist, exposing her full breasts and rosy nipples. His gaze remained fixed on hers as he trailed his fingertips down either side of the smooth column of her neck, to where it curved into her shoulders.

She trembled. "What else?"

"Well, there are the obvious hot spots." He plucked the ripe tip of one nipple and drew a gasp from her passion-swollen lips before trailing a fingertip under the fullness of one breast, over the few inches of exposed skin until he reached the material bunched at her waist. He eased his fingers inside and pushed the dress over her hips until it slid down her legs. He stroked her bare mound with the pad of his thumb and watched her gaze darken.

"And then there are the not-so-obvious." He dropped to his knees and unfastened her shoes. His fingers lingered at the tender arch of one foot after he removed her shoes. "The feet are packed with nerve endings." He stroked the inside from her ankle to her toes before cupping her ankles with either hand and massaging gently.

"That does feel good."

"Just good?" He worked his way up her calves, the backs of her knees, her thighs, until he reached her sweet ass. He kneaded her, teasing the seam with his fingertips until she moaned.

"I've thought about touching you like this so many times since that night down by the river," he told her. "Too many times."

"I've thought about it, too."

He glanced up and caught her gaze. Her eyes were bright blue, fueled with desire and a dozen other emotions he couldn't name.

But he wanted to.

He wanted to know what she was thinking. Everything she was thinking.

"If you were dreaming this up right now, if this were your fantasy come to life, what would happen next? What would you *want* to happen next?"

Her expression seemed suddenly guarded and he knew he'd guessed at least some of what was going on in her head. "I thought we were doing erogenous zones, not Fantasy 101?"

"Trust me, there will be plenty of erogenous zones involved in what we're about to do."

"And what are we about to do?"

"You tell me." He cupped her face. "In your most erotic thoughts, what happens next?"

She didn't even have to think. "You pick me up

and carry me into the shower. We soap each other or we kiss. Or both."

He gave her a slow, lazy grin that made her blush despite her boldness. "I'll see what I can do." He stood, picked her up and stepped into the shower.

The door closed and the steam engulfed them. Hot water pelted his back and flowed over his skin. Easing her to her feet, he enjoyed the slow glide of her body down the slick, hard length of his.

"Turn around."

Deanie heard his deep voice, but she couldn't seem to comply. She'd pictured just this situation before and she was anxious to see if it lived up to her imagination.

Her gaze swept the length of him. His broad shoulders framed a wide chest sprinkled with crisp, dark hair that stretched from nipple to nipple in a V-shape. The brown silk narrowed and funneled down his abdomen and pelvis to disappear in the thatch of dark hair that surrounded his massive erection. His legs were braced apart, his thigh muscles taut, sprinkled with the same dark hair that covered his chest. His gaze was liquid gold and just as mesmerizing.

His big, powerful form filled up the shower stall and blocked the spray of water. Water hammered the back of his head and ran in tiny rivulets over his shoulders down his chest and abdomen to drip-drop off his swollen testicles.

She watched as he reached for the soap. He rubbed the bar between his large hands. Lather squeezed between his fingers and trailed down his powerful forearms.

"Turn around," he said again.

She obeyed this time and he stepped up behind her. She glanced down as his arms came around. His dark hands spread the white lather over her pale stomach. He cupped her breasts and slicked the soap over her nipples. She gasped.

"See? I told you we wouldn't forget about the erogenous zones." He plucked and rolled the hard peaks until she trembled with sensation.

He paused then to reach for the soap. He didn't just lather his hands this time. Instead, he slid the bar down her quivering stomach, over the bare flesh of her sex.

"You're so soft and smooth," he murmured, his voice as thick as the erection pressing into the cleft of her buttocks.

All of a sudden, the humiliation and pain involved with a full "beauty" session at the hands of Romeo's one and only waxing specialist—Miss Ethel from Ethel's Day Spa—seemed a small price to pay for Rance's admiration.

He stroked her, rubbing the bar of soap in a sweet circular motion before moving down between her legs.

"Spread your legs for me." She widened her stance, giving him better access. The hard edge slid along the soft folds between her legs. The soap brushed her throbbing clitoris and intense pleasure rushed through her.

"Is this what happens in your fantasy?"

"No." He went still and her body hummed in expectancy. "It's better than any fantasy. Sweeter. Sharper. More intense." She felt his muscles ease. And then he moved, doing wickedly delicious things with the soap that told her he'd not only been waiting for her response, but he'd liked it.

A lot.

HE SOAPED her from head to toe, giving extra attention to every hot spot until Deanie shook with a need so fierce she couldn't stand it. She turned in his arms, desperate to feel him.

She touched everywhere she could reach, slicking her palms up and down his hard shoulders and hair-roughened chest. His taut hips and muscular buttocks. When she cupped his testicles, he growled.

He turned and flipped the water off. He grabbed

a towel from a nearby shelf and hooked it around her neck. Where the past few moments had been wild and fast, the brakes came on and everything slowed to a nice and easy and nerve-racking pace.

The fluffy white towel moved over her aroused body with an incredible slowness that made her want to scream. She didn't. Just when she thought she couldn't take any more, he pulled away. He wiped the moisture from his own body, scrubbed at his damp hair and then tossed the towel to the floor.

Before Deanie could draw breath, he reached for her. He pulled her flush against him. His hard length pressed into her stomach and he rubbed himself while his mouth devoured her in a deep, lusty kiss that made her insides clench and her nipples tingle.

Gripping her buttocks, he lifted her. She wrapped her legs around his waist and her arms around his neck. His hard, pulsing flesh grazed the sensitive area between her legs. The length rubbed against her slick folds as he turned and stepped from the shower stall.

He kept kissing her as he walked the few feet from the bathroom to the bedroom and eased her down on the king-size mattress.

Rounding the end of the bed, he grasped the shorts he'd shed. His shoulders bunched and his muscles flexed as he leaned down and retrieved a small foil packet from his pocket. He came to stand beside the bed, towering over her as he rolled the condom down his thick length with a swiftness that amazed her.

In that next instant, he was right where she wanted him, between her legs, his weight pressing her back into the mattress. His erection slid along her damp flesh, making her shudder and moan and arch toward him. He slid his hands beneath her, gripped her bottom and tilted her to take all of him. He plunged deep.

A shudder ripped through him and she touched him, trailing her hands over his hard buttocks, pulling him more securely inside. Her body clasped him, convulsing and quivering when he finally retreated. But he didn't leave her empty for long. He thrust into her again and again, building the pressure and pushing them both higher until, finally, he sent her soaring.

Deanie cried out Rance's name and dug her nails into his hard muscles as a wave of ecstasy washed over her. A tidal wave, it seemed, because the sensation went on and on, drenching her senses until she was left floating.

She opened her eyes to find Rance poised above her, a fierce look on his face, his eyes gleaming with an intensity that reached inside of her and tugged at her heart.

When she gave him a blissful smile, he pounded into her one final time and let himself go. Every muscle in his body went rigid and his deep groan echoed in her ears.

He rolled over without breaking their intimate contact and cradled her on his chest, her head nestled in the curve of his shoulder. Large hands stroked up and down her back in a reverent motion that brought tears to Deanie's eyes.

But she didn't cry. There would be plenty of time for that tomorrow when she said her goodbyes and walked away from Rance.

For now, she held tight to the joy that rippled through her and focused on the man beneath her, the warmth of his neck against her cheek, the steady thud of his heart against her breast, the feel of his powerful arms locked around her.

This man. This moment. *This*.

12

THE SUN WAS just coming up when Rance opened his eyes. He felt Deanie's warmth next to him, her bottom nestled against his penis, her back flush against his chest, her full breasts cushioned by the arm he'd tucked around her. She sighed, snuggling more securely against him. The sound echoed in his head, making his blood thrum and his heart beat faster. His senses felt alive with the sight, the sound, the taste, the feel of her.

He felt alive.

A wave of pure satisfaction rushed through him. It was a feeling unlike anything he'd ever felt before. With any woman. Any competition.

Shit.

Rance eased away from her and swung his legs over the edge of the bed. He pushed to his feet and paced to the French doors. He hauled open the door and the morning breeze wafted in, but it provided little relief to his hot body.

Hot, of all the friggin' things. His skin itched and his muscles bunched and his dick twitched in memory of the past night and the awesome sex. And damned if he didn't want more.

What had happened to working her out of his system?

He raked a hand through his hair and fixed his gaze on the breathtaking view. Orange fingers of light played across the horizon and cast fiery rays on the glasslike water. The beach was practically deserted except for the small group making their way toward the far end and the marina.

Erica. Rance knew it was her even before he spotted her familiar blond hair. He remembered her invite and his promise to join her and her group of friends. Oddly enough, he didn't feel the usual rush of adrenaline at the idea of climbing onto a wakeboard and riding hell-bent for leather across the ocean.

His heart didn't pound and his pulse didn't race and he didn't feel the slightest bit of excitement at the prospect.

Rather, he yearned to crawl back between the sheets, pull Deanie into his arms and kiss every inch of her body until she opened her eyes and smiled at him.

Holy shit.

He walked back into the room and retrieved a spare set of clothes he'd purchased at the clothing store downstairs. He pulled on the army green board shorts and did his best to ignore the inviting picture Deanie made curled on her side, her delectable bottom facing him.

He wasn't going to scoot up next to her, gather her close and drink in the intoxicating aroma of her—

The thought stalled as she rolled onto her back. The sheets twisted, tugging down around her waist as she moved to reveal her pale breasts tipped with taut, rose-colored nipples. Her dark hair lay spread out on the crisp white pillow. Her eyes were closed, her face calm and serene. Her full lips were pink and swollen from his kisses. She looked so beautiful and sexy lying in his bed.

His.

Rance braced himself against the notion, yanked on his T-shirt, and stuffed his feet into flip-flops.

And then Rance did the only thing he'd ever done where Deanie Codge was concerned.

He walked away.

"I TOLD YOU HE'D COME." Erica turned a smile on Rance when he approached the group gathered on the dock. Every gaze swiveled toward him and a handful of smiles erupted.

"This is Rachel and Buster." Erica started introducing the young men and women who surrounded her. They were all young—early twenties maybe. They looked typical of the radical sports set with their trendy hair and multiple piercings. "Carrie and Sue." She pointed to two women who wore navy blue wet suits. One had a buzz cut with a dozen earrings lining one ear, while the other wore her long hair in dozens of tiny braids. A stud glittered from her nose.

"And this is my boyfriend, Zee," Erica added as she pointed to the young man just to her left. Where the others had been all smiles and eager hand shakes, the tall, muscular blonde—the ends of his short, spiked hair died a dark black—merely gave a quick nod.

"Zee's the best wakeboarder on the island," Erica went on. "That is, until you arrived. Man-o-man, I can't believe you're actually here."

"It's an honor, Mr. McGraw," Buster said, stepping forward. "You're, like, my idol, dude. I saw you dive into those sharks last year when you did that freestyle skiing competition in Hawaii. Awesome. Totally awesome."

"There are plenty of sharks around these waters," Zee said as he zipped up the vest of his wetsuit. "We're neck deep in them all the time."

"You totally rocked in the base jumping finals over in Peru." The comment came from one of the women. "You made even the hardest jump look easy."

"Thanks," Rance said. "It's all about staying focused and—"

"We do some base jumping over by the cliffs," Zee cut in, obviously not the least bit interested in Rance's advice. He popped open a can of sex wax and started to rub down his board. "It's not that big of a deal."

"That snake wrangling thing last year was way rad," Carrie said. "I watched it on ESPN with my brother," she motioned to Buster "and the both of us nearly peed our pants. But you were cool, man. You didn't even flinch, much less look scared."

Obviously, Zee hadn't done much snake wrangling, because he didn't comment. Instead, he shoved the lid onto the can of wax, picked up his board and said, "Are we going to stand here on the dock and run our mouths all day, or are we going to thrash some waves?"

"He takes his waves seriously," Erica told Rance once Zee had climbed into the boat and out of earshot.

"He should. That's what it takes to make a winner."

Rance knew that firsthand because he'd always taken things seriously. He'd approached each and every competition with the serious intent of winning, and he always had.

Until now.

Like hell, buddy.

Okay, so he'd stopped giving it his all some time ago, but he'd managed to fake it because he was a competitor by nature and so he'd kept up his winning streak. He knew how to intimidate his opponents and how to keep his game face. He'd learned that early on when he'd tackled steers with Clay. It was all about showing the other guy who was boss and acting before your opponent could react. He'd relied on speed and stamina and heart.

An image of Deanie pushed into his head, but he pushed it right back out. He wasn't getting sidetracked, and he sure as hell wasn't letting a few doubts undermine the career he'd spent a lifetime building. While each competition seemed harder and harder—and much more outrageous—he wasn't going to let it undermine his determination. The key was not to give up.

Not to walk away.

No matter how much his gut ached to do just that.

Rance summoned the competitive nature that had lived and breathed inside of him for so long and stepped onto the boat. He took the spare wet suit Erica retrieved from a compartment near the stern of the boat and headed for the small cabin. A few minutes later, he emerged, dressed and ready for action.

He *was* ready, he told himself. Even if the notion of climbing into the water and onto the board didn't stir even a quarter of the excitement it once had.

He was tired. Exhausted. In a good way, of course—the sex had been incredible. But exhausted just the same. Of course, he wouldn't be into it as intensely as someone like, say, Zee, who'd probably had a full night's sleep.

The boat roared to life and they headed for open water. Fifteen minutes later, they slowed to an idle. Zee dropped over the side of the boat with his wakeboard. Erica took her place behind the wheel, revved the gas and the boat roared to life.

Behind them, Zee climbed onto the small surfing apparatus, knees bent, arms tight as he gripped the rope that trailed from the back of the boat. The boat quickly took up the rope's slack and jerked it tight. Water kicked up and so did Zee as he held on and trailed behind.

The speed increased and Zee went into action. He veered this way and that. He rocked onto his side and flipped up into the air and proved beyond a doubt why the locals considered him the best. He was every bit as good as Rance had once been.

Maybe even better.

Like hell. That should have been his first thought. That had *always* been the first thought whenever he'd seen someone better or stronger or hungrier.

Not anymore.

Because you're just not that into it. It isn't your passion. It never has been.

The truth echoed in his head as the boat slowed to a halt again. Zee raised a victory hand before jumping off the board into the calming water and excitement echoed among the group.

"Kick ass!"

"That's the way to do it!"

"Totally rad!"

"He's good, isn't he?" Erica left the engine idling and came up beside Rance.

"Very good."

"You should see him on a surfboard. Or skis. Or with a parasail. You name it, he can do it. We all can," she added. "Just not quite as good as him."

"Is that right?" Rance eyed the young man and an idea struck.

A crazy idea that he dismissed immediately.

Zee, board under one arm, swam the few feet

to the back of the boat and hauled himself up the ladder. He gave Rance a smug, bring-it-on look before taking his place behind the boat's wheel and gunning the engine for the next person.

"Why don't you hit the water?" Erica's eyes danced with excitement. "We'd love to see you in action."

"You guys go first." He motioned to the handful of people around him. "Then I'll do my thing." He would, he told himself, no matter how his muscles ached or how tired he felt. A little wakeboarding was sure to pump him up for the flight to Australia and the competition that awaited him.

And if it didn't?

It didn't matter. He was still going. Regardless of the fact that his heart wasn't in it anymore and he couldn't stop thinking about Deanie and he had a sudden hankering for his aunt Lurline's blueberry cobbler.

Rance McGraw couldn't just piss it all away.

"So that's it? You're just going to piss it all away? Just like that?" Shank asked when Rance called him later that morning.

It was close to ten o'clock and Rance sat in the lobby of the hotel where he'd been for the past few hours trying to work out the details of the crazy idea he'd had earlier while watching Zee and the others. An energy drink sat on the table next to him, courtesy of one of the numerous hotel staff that hustled around him. The place had already come to life. Guests walked here and there, some headed for the pool, others for the beach.

Deanie wasn't among them.

She was still curled up in his bed, sound asleep. He'd checked on her after he'd finished with Erica and Zee. He'd been anxious to share his latest brainstorm, but she'd looked so peaceful and content that he'd merely tucked the sheet around her and given her a soft, lingering kiss.

They would have plenty of time to talk once he'd worked out all the details.

"I'm not pissing anything away," Rance told his business partner. "I'm stepping down as spokesperson for Extreme Dream and letting you take full control of the company. I'll be a silent partner." His voice grew softer, more serious. "I can't do it anymore, Shank. I don't *want* to do it. I want to go home."

Silence settled on the line before Shank finally spoke. "Well, it's about damned time."

"I don't mean to leave you high and dry. I've already worked out a deal for a new spokesperson, or rather, a team of them—what did you say?"

"I said it's about damned time. I'm sick of seeing you live out of a suitcase. Sure, it's been good for business. As your partner, I can't complain. But as your friend, I can't tell you how many times I've been tempted to fire your ass and hire someone else because you were too stubborn to at least slow down a little."

"How come you never said anything?"

"Would it have done any good?" Without waiting for a reply, Shank went on. "You forget that I've known you a helluva long time. Now tell me about this extreme dream team you've got planned that's going to make us both even richer than we already are…"

WHEN DEANIE finally forced her eyes open, sunlight streamed through the window. Her thighs ached and her nipples tingled as she forced herself to a sitting position. She blinked once, twice against the fog of sleep and then glanced at the clock.

Her gaze didn't make it past the cowboy hat that sat on the nightstand. The previous night rushed at her.

Sex, she told herself as the images played in her head.

But truthfully, it had been more.

The proof lay in the way her stomach fluttered and her heart pounded when she remembered. And the sudden rush of loneliness that swamped her as she stared at the empty spot next to her.

It was a feeling she knew all too well.

No!

Panic gripped her and pumped her heart faster. Deanie bolted to her feet and rushed around the room, searching frantically for her clothes. She blinked back the tears that burned her eyes and fought to get a grip on the emotion pushing and pulling inside her.

She wasn't doing this again.

There would be no falling apart, no moping around, no feeling her heart shatter into a million pieces because her heart was not—repeat *not*—involved. Last night had been wonderful, but it was over. She was going to handle the situation like a mature adult, get herself together, and get the hell out of Rance's room before he came back and made her decision that much harder.

When he touched her, he stirred too many memories and she started to fall in love with him all over again.

Fall, mind you. She wasn't actually *in* love.

Not completely.

Not yet.

Which meant she could still get out of the situation without making a complete idiot of herself.

Yanking on her clothes, Deanie slipped from his room and headed down the hallway for the elevator.

With her shoes dangling from one hand, she punched the elevator button and prayed with all of her heart when the doors finally opened that she wouldn't come face-to-face with him.

Obviously someone upstairs was listening because the doors slid open and no Rance.

Instead, Deanie found herself staring at a very old, very naked man.

RANCE HAD NEVER felt better in his entire life.

He decided as much when he hung up the phone with Romeo's one and only real estate attorney. Not only had Rance found the woman of his dreams but, as of five seconds ago, he'd offered an obscene amount of money to the new owner of Romeo's old rodeo arena and taken the first official step back home.

Excitement pulsed through him as he headed through the lobby toward the gift shop to pick up something for Deanie.

He was just about to turn when someone let out a shriek. He whirled just in time to see a woman sprint past him. She had snow white hair and pale skin.

A *lot* of pale skin.

From her head to her toes, and every naked inch in between.

"That's her!" someone shouted. "That's the streaker!"

A half dozen security guards bounded through the lobby after her, but they were too late. She'd already disappeared through the double glass doors.

Rance quickly found himself rounded up as one of the witnesses and ushered toward the security office.

He was just about to pull open the door when someone pushed it open from the inside.

"Deanie."

At the sound of her name, her head jerked up and her gaze collided with his. Joy flashed in her green eyes for one fast, furious heartbeat and Rance felt his own heart kick into action.

"What are you doing here?" she asked him.

"I'm about to give a statement. That streaker damn near ran me over in the lobby."

"I saw him, too. All of him this time. But it was on the elevator. I just gave a description."

"Him? But it was a her." Not that it mattered.

All that mattered was the woman standing in front of him. "I really need to talk to you—"

"Can you two do this later?" The tall, beefy head of security came up behind Rance and motioned him inside the office. "I've got a lot of people to talk to."

"Just a second," Rance told the man. "This is important. Deanie." He turned back to her. "About last night—"

"You shouldn't keep Mr. H. waiting," she blurted. "The sooner he can catch this guy, the safer everyone will be."

"Guy? It's a woman, honey."

"Whatever. Look, you go on and do what you need to do."

"But I just want to say—"

"We'll talk later," she cut in. "*Go.* I've got to get going myself. I've got a few things to do." She darted past him and headed for the elevator.

"Meet me in my hotel room."

She didn't answer or spare him another glance.

An uneasy feeling settled in the pit of Rance's stomach and he had the crazy urge to run after her, haul her into his arms and kiss her goodbye.

Goodbye?

It wasn't goodbye. Not this time. Rance McGraw wasn't going anywhere except right back where he belonged, and he was taking Deanie Codge with him.

After last night, he had no doubt that she still had feelings for him. And now she knew he had feelings for her. It was just a matter of working out the details.

DEANIE HANDED what little she had over to the concierge and tried to calm the anxiety that had followed her since she'd run into Rance. And the guilt.

She hadn't actually said she'd meet him, she reminded herself. She hadn't said anything. She'd just rushed up to her own room, gathered her things and rushed back downstairs to check out before he finished his meeting with the security officer.

Coward.

Maybe so. But she preferred the term self-preservationist. She glanced at her watch before chancing a look around. No Rance. No naked men. Just a very sad looking Savannah Sierra Ellington.

The young woman sat on a nearby sofa, her eyes red and swollen. Her cheeks puffy. Tiny black streaks of mascara trailed down her face.

"Savannah?" Deanie sank down next to the woman.

She glanced up, her blue eyes watery. As if she'd been caught with her hand in the cookie jar, she smiled and wiped frantically at her face. "Hey, there... Deanie, isn't it?"

Deanie nodded. "Are you okay?"

"Why, certainly." She set the cell phone she'd been holding aside and pulled a tissue from her designer purse. "I'm just a little tired."

"Big night last night?"

"You bet." She pulled out a compact and flipped it open. "My word, would you look what the cat dragged in? It's a shame what a dozen margaritas and a night of dancing will do to you."

"So you had fun?"

"Why wouldn't I?" She hesitated as she stared into the mirror. "I'm single and carefree and I danced with oodles of men last night. I certainly don't need that lowdown, no-good, two-timing boyfriend of mine."

"The one who cancelled on you at the last minute?"

"That's the one." Her expression faltered and she stared at her hands. "It really wasn't all that last minute. He hasn't called in two weeks. That right there should have told me he wasn't interested. But I kept telling myself he was just busy. Turns out, he's a jerk."

"I'm so sorry."

She shrugged and tried for another smile. "But

what the hey, right? Easy come, easy go. I'm not letting him mess up my vacation. There's plenty more where he came from."

That's the trouble, Deanie thought as she watched Savannah pull a tissue from her purse, wipe her cheeks and head for the ladies' room. There were plenty more jerks out there and Savannah would undoubtedly find another one before she could down her next margarita.

She'd find another and he would treat her bad because that's how she expected to be treated. Despite her I'm-all-that attitude and her hot clothes, she didn't feel all that hot deep down inside.

Deanie had seen the insecurity in her eyes when she'd stared into the compact mirror, and she'd recognized it.

Because Deanie had felt the same inadequacy.

The same longing to be good enough. Pretty enough. Woman enough.

"Your cab's here." The concierge's voice drew her around and Deanie started for the front glass doors and the cab that had just pulled up to the curb.

A handsome man in his sixties, impeccably dressed in a designer suit, climbed out and pulled a money clip the size of Texas from his wallet just as Deanie pushed through the rotating doors. He peeled off a hundred dollar bill, murmured "Keep the change," to the driver and turned to run smack-dab into Deanie.

"Excuse me," he exclaimed as her purse hit the ground, along with the small bag of clothes she'd purchased yesterday. "I didn't see you." He dropped to his knees at the same time that Deanie did to help her gather up her things. "I usually watch where I'm going, but I'm just so late."

"A business meeting?" Deanie asked as she gathered up several tubes of lipstick that had spilled out of her purse.

"I'm meeting someone. *The* someone." His brown eyes started to shine and he paused, his hand stalled on Deanie's new sundress which had spilled from the bag. "She's the most wonderful someone in the world and the most patient. I swear, I don't deserve the likes of Mavoreen."

"Mavoreen Rosenbaum?" When he nodded, Deanie blurted, "You're the billionaire."

His eyes took on an excited gleam. "Do you know her?"

"We met on the plane."

"And she mentioned me?" When Deanie nodded, he smiled. "Isn't she an extraordinary woman? A pearl among old, corroded oyster beds. A diamond swimming in a sea of cubic zirconia."

"Mavoreen?"

He stared at Deanie, his expression serious. "I know she might not be the most beautiful at first glance, but she's got this confidence. You know, I've dated supermodels. Actresses. Wealthy women with the best plastic surgeons. They all had looks, but nothing to back it up. They were beautiful, but they didn't feel beautiful. Mavoreen feels it, and it makes her beautiful." He shook his head. "I really should get going. I don't want to keep her waiting any longer than necessary. I've written a poem for her and I can't wait to read it."

Deanie smiled as she watched the man disappear into the lobby.

It seemed as if Mavoreen wasn't all that delusional after all.

"Are you ready, ma'am?"

Deanie turned at the sound of the cab driver's voice.

She wasn't delusional either. Maybe Mavoreen had beaten the odds, but she was the one and only. For the most part, exceptional men like Rance didn't fall head over heels for not-so-exceptional women like Deanie.

Not then.

And certainly not now.

Deanie climbed into the cab.

THE UNEASINESS RANCE had felt stayed with him as he gave his statement to the security officer and fielded several phone calls from Shank and the real estate attorney. It took a half hour before he finished with everything and returned to his hotel room, and he felt every agonizing second.

"Happy Valentine's Day," he called out when he opened the door.

He stepped inside the room, only to find it empty.

His hat still sat on the nightstand next to the bed. He set the bouquet of roses he'd picked up downstairs on the tangled mass of sheets. Visions of silky arms and long legs wrapped around him flashed in his mind. Heat skimmed over his flesh, but it didn't warm the fist of coldness that had settled in the pit of his stomach.

Turning, Rance made a visual search of the room again, all the while fighting against the truth that niggled at his gut.

She was gone.

Maybe not. Maybe she's in her own hotel room waiting for you.

But he knew she'd left even as he dialed the front desk. He felt it in the slow thud of his heart and the ache in his chest and the damned loneliness that wrapped around him and tightened like one of those giant snakes he'd tangled with during his last competition.

"You just missed her, Mr. McGraw," the concierge said. "I loaded her into a cab myself. She's halfway to the airport by now."

Rance let the receiver slide into place, his arms suddenly heavier than they'd felt in a long, long time. He tried to swallow, but his throat felt tight. His gut ached and he couldn't seem to catch his breath. For the first time, he understood how Deanie had felt that day he'd left her behind.

Her hurt. Her disappointment.

The realization gripped him for several heart-pounding moments, and then he did what she hadn't done all those years ago when he'd been the one to leave.

He went after her.

_13_

"WHERE ARE YOU GOING?" Rance's voice slid into Deanie's ears as she took her boarding pass from the attendant at the terminal desk.

"To Eden. As planned." She started toward the doorway that opened up onto the runway.

The plane sat several feet away, the door open, the portable staircase firmly attached. People climbed the stairs, boarding the plane that would make its next stop in Eden before returning to Miami.

"Deanie." Her name sounded a heartbeat before he caught her arm in a firm grip and brought her whirling around to face him. "Stop. Just stop."

"I can't." She did her best to look anywhere, everywhere but into his mesmerizing gaze. "They're boarding."

He caught her face between his hands. "We need to talk." Determination glittered in his eyes, along with something else.

Something fierce and possessive and…
No.

It couldn't be.

She fought down the hope that blossomed inside of her and held tight to the anger and humiliation she'd felt the day he'd stuffed his suitcases in the back of Clay's old pickup and climbed into the passenger's seat without so much as a backwards glance.

Her brother had driven him to the airport that day where he'd boarded a plane for Texas A&M and the football scholarship that awaited him. She'd watched the truck turn into a cloud of dust on the horizon and then she'd cried so hard her eyes had been swollen for days.

But her heart had hurt even longer.

Because she'd let it, she reminded herself. She'd practically handed it to him on a silver platter to do with as he pleased.

Not this time.

She'd offered her body last night, but her heart was still her own and she intended to guard it, to fight for it.

"Look, Rance, you don't owe me anything. I'm a big girl. I know that last night was just sex."

"It was just sex." His hands fell away from her

face and he caught her free hand with one of his. "Incredible sex. The best sex of my life."

"Meaning?"

"You can't get on that plane." When she started to protest, his fingers tightened around hers. "You don't need Camp E.D.E.N. You're a sexy, beautiful, desirable woman. The past twenty-four hours proves it."

"Maybe, but now it's over. You get on with your plans and I get on with mine. Isn't that what you had in mind yesterday? Deal with me and get on with your life?"

"Yes, but—"

"But what?"

"It's not that simple anymore."

"It is." She blinked back the tears that suddenly threatened to overwhelm her. "Let go. Please."

His grip loosened, but he didn't release her. "I'm not going to Australia. I'm going back home to Romeo."

"And?" She fought against the hope that refused to let loose of her.

He was going *home*.

Now.

Finally.

Meanwhile, Deanie was headed for Dallas and the rest of her new life.

"Didn't you hear me?" He touched her cheek with his free hand. "I'm moving back to Romeo."

Strong fingers played across her cheek and she barely resisted the urge to turn her face into his palm. "What about Extreme Dream?"

"I'll still be a partner. A silent partner." He let his hand fall away and shook his head. "I can't do it anymore. Alligator wrestling isn't for me. Just like football wasn't for me. Not really. I was good at it, but only because I was strong and determined and I could take a man down in no time flat. And that," he told her, "came from rolling around in a rodeo arena all those years while I was growing up. Football was just convenient. A way to use the skills I'd already developed." His gaze darkened. "It was a way out. My only way out, but it wasn't my passion."

"Steer wrestling," she said and he nodded. "So you're going back to Romeo to wrestle steers?"

"In a manner of speaking. I made a few phone calls this morning and I bought the old rodeo arena."

"That's about to be a shopping center."

"Not as of twenty minutes ago. The new owner has already accepted my offer." His eyes glittered with that wild, passionate light she remembered so well from their childhood. "I'm going to renovate the entire place and host rodeo events. During the down time, I'll utilize it as a training facility for cowboys of all ages and offer different classes for the various events." He grinned and her heart fluttered. "Kids can practice out there just the way Clay and I used to do."

The statement stirred a memory and Deanie saw herself sitting on the sidelines, watching Rance and hoping with all of her heart for a wave or a smile or even a friendly nod of his head.

The image morphed and the young girl transformed into an adult. Deanie saw herself now, sitting there in her fancy sundress and higher-than-should-be-legally-allowed high heels. But even though she was grown up and different, she still wore the same desperate look of longing for a man she loved with all her heart.

A man who didn't love her back.

"Good luck to you," she told him, swallowing against the lump in her throat. "I hope everything works out."

He shook his head. "Didn't you hear me? I'm going home. I'll be right there in Romeo. We'll see each other every day."

"No, we won't. I live in Dallas now. I've got a job there and I already leased an apartment—"

"So break the lease. You don't belong in Dallas. You hate traffic and concrete and malls. And Dallas is loaded with all three."

"I've actually developed quite a fondness for malls. I've been to the one in Austin at least six times over the past month. I'm sure I'll get used to the rest."

"The way you've gotten used to the do-me shoes." He glanced down at the flip-flops she'd slid on in her rush to checkout of the hotel and make her flight.

"I'm in a hurry and I can't walk as fast in them. But that doesn't mean I don't *like* them. Or that they hurt my feet in any way, shape or form. I've really got to go." She pulled away from him and headed across the pavement toward the staircase that led to the plane.

"Don't do this, Deanie. Don't get on that plane. Please." The word was soft, but it packed a powerful punch that she felt between her rib cage. "You belong in Romeo."

She did.

She knew it deep down inside and it stirred her fear and panic and made her pick up her steps.

Because Deanie didn't want to go back to her old life. She didn't want to find herself back in

Romeo, lusting after a man who didn't love her. Things would be a little different now because he returned that lust—the past twenty-four hours proved it—but everyone knew that lust faded.

She didn't want to wind up sitting on that corral fence, waiting and hoping for him to glance her way.

"You belong with me."

His deep, desperate voice stalled Deanie just shy of the first step. Her fingers tightened on the hand rail and her breath caught and she knew what he was going to say even before the words slid into her ears.

"I love you."

"Love?" She turned on him. "We've been together all of twenty-four hours and now you think you love me?"

"We've been together a lifetime and I *know* I love you." His fierce gaze caught and held hers as he crossed the distance to her. "I've always loved you, I just didn't realize it." He came up to her, so close that his shadow blocked the sun that blazed overhead. "I was too lost in my own problems. Too mad at the world because I'd lost my parents and my home. But I still had you. You were there for me. You made me want to wake up every morning because I knew I'd see you on the bus. I knew you'd be there."

All the pain and heartache she'd felt in the past paled in comparison to the pure joy that rushed through her at that moment. She wanted to think that he was just saying the words to stop her from getting on the plane, to fulfill his promise to her brother.

But she knew better.

She'd felt the proof last night when he'd held her so tenderly, so possessively in his arms. And she saw the proof now in the fierce light that gleamed in his gaze.

He really and truly *loved* her.

And she loved him.

She always had.

She'd loved him more than she'd ever loved anyone or anything. More than her favorite horse or a brand-new computerized transmission. More than her pride. More than her ego. More than herself.

The realization hit her as she stood there in his shadow, the hot pavement seeping up through the soles of her flip-flops.

"I love you, too," she told him, and then she turned and mounted the steps leading to the plane.

"You're running away," he said, but he didn't reach for her. His voice followed her up the steps. "You're scared and you're running."

He was right. She *was* running.

But not from him.

Deanie was running from herself. From the tomboy who'd never been good enough personally or professionally or sexually.

She would always be running unless she changed the things about herself that had marked her for failure from the very beginning. She had to finish what she'd started.

Wiping frantically at a tear that squeezed past her lashes, she ignored the concerned look of the flight attendant as she topped the staircase and walked on board the plane. A few seconds later, she sank down in a window seat and took a deep, shaking breath.

She'd done it. *She'd* walked away this time, and taken her heart with her.

So why did she feel as if someone had reached inside of her and ripped it out?

Wiping at a sudden flood of hot tears, she blinked frantically and tried to focus on her surroundings. The plane looked the same as the one she'd been on yesterday, from the cheesy heart-shaped cutouts to the red and white streamers in honor of Valentine's Day.

Today.

Deanie was no worse off today than she'd been on any other V-day in her past, yet she felt even emptier. Lonelier.

Better to have loved and lost than never to have loved at all...

Yeah, right.

She chanced a glance out the window to see Rance standing where she'd left him, staring at the plane, his fists clenched, his body taut, as if it took all his strength not to barrel up the steps after her.

It was an image that stayed rooted in her mind as she fastened her seat belt and waited for takeoff.

"DO YOU MIND if we sit next to you?"

The question drew Deanie from her thoughts and she glanced up to see an elderly woman wearing a beige polyester pantsuit and a matching scarf.

The plane had just turned to taxi down the runway. The aircraft trembled as it moved across the pavement and the woman held the back of one seat to brace herself. She smiled, her face crinkling, and Deanie found herself reminded of Miss Margie and all the other senior ladies who'd been her loyal customers over the years.

Her chest tightened.

"My husband and I both have terrible allergies," the woman went on, "and the lady sitting on our row has cat hair all over her sweater."

"I don't mind at all," Deanie said just as the flight attendant walked up to them.

"Take your seats, please," the young woman said. "We're about to taxi the runway."

"We're just about to." The old woman signaled to her husband who still sat a few rows back. "It's okay, dear. Hurry up and don't forget to bring my purse." She angled sideways and took the seat next to Deanie. "There." She fastened her seat belt. "Now I can breathe again. So," she turned to Deanie. "Are you headed to Eden or back to Miami?"

"Eden. I got off to take a breather yesterday when we reached Escapades and the plane took off without me."

"How terrible. But hopefully you enjoyed your stay at Escapades. It's a beautiful island. My husband and I always stop off on our way to Eden."

"You're headed there? I didn't think they allowed couples. I thought it was strictly for individuals."

"It is. We're not students, dear. We're instructors. I have a masters in social psychology from the University of California at Berkeley, and Marvin, my dear sweet husband, has his doctorate in human sexuality. We teach a seminar on the sexual excitement of public exposure."

"Come again?"

"Streaking, dear. Our seminar is about streaking." Just as she said the words, her husband collapsed in the seat next to her.

Deanie stared at the familiar face that turned toward her—a face she'd seen not a few hours ago, along with all the rest of him—and realization hit her.

There had been two streakers at Escapades, and they were now both sitting next to her.

"Streaking?" Deanie cleared her throat and tried not to blush as she smiled at Dr. Marvin. "How, um, exactly does that fit with the whole getting in touch with your own sexuality premise?"

"For some individuals, there is no pleasure in actual intercourse. Some people are just too inhibited to share such an intimate act with a partner. Right, Marvin?" He grunted, settling back into his chair as if all were right with the world and Deanie hadn't seen him in his birthday suit.

"Or maybe," the woman went on, "they simply don't have an available partner. Or, as is our case, maybe they're just too old to enjoy traditional sex. Marvin, dear that he is, hasn't had an erection in a long time. Likewise, I can't even remember what an orgasm feels like. But that doesn't mean we have to lead boring lives sexually. We can still feel the same rush of excitement that we used to without actual *doing* anything."

"Except streaking?"

"Exactly. The thrill of being out in the open can stimulate the heart and bloodstream as much as an actual sexual encounter."

Deanie thought back to last night and the beach and Rance. She'd been out in the open and very excited even before she'd touched him and he'd touched her. Likewise, she'd been completely turned on when he'd touched her earlier at the pool.

But it was one thing to get worked up over the *possibility* of discovery and quite another to strip naked and openly flash her goodies to anyone who happened by.

Or, in Professor Marvin's case, to openly flop it at anyone who happened by.

"Not to mention," the old woman went on, "there's the added bonus of sharing yourself with more than one person. Group encounters can be very healthy and enlightening. You'll learn more about that when you reach Eden…"

The engine roared and the plane started down

the runway. Deanie clutched the arms of her seat and did her best to ignore the hollowness in the pit of her stomach. And her chest.

Instead, she focused on the old woman who went on to fill Deanie in on the health benefits—both mental and physical—of publicly exposing one's self.

What the hell am I doing?

The thought struck fifteen minutes later as they started their descent.

You're changing. Evolving. Getting in touch with your inner female.

The trouble was, Deanie's inner female wasn't any more enlightened than her outer female. If getting in touch with her sexuality meant streaking buck naked through a crowd of people, then she was doomed to stay out of touch.

No way was Deanie shedding her clothes in front of a classroom of people, not even for education's sake.

Some might call her naive and unsophisticated, and they would be right. Deanie was both.

She still believed in one man and one woman. She believed in love and commitment and romance and leaving a few things to the imagination. And she knew, deep down inside, that no makeover, no matter how extreme, was going to change that.

"Aren't you getting off?" the old woman asked when they rolled to a stop and she and her husband stood to file off the plane.

"No, ma'am." Deanie refastened her seat belt. "I'm going home."

RANCE STOOD OUT in front of the Feed-n-Seed in downtown Romeo and stared across the street. It was only February, but the air was already starting to heat up, foreshadowing the blistering summer that would soon follow. A drop of perspiration slid down Rance's temple, but the heat gripping him had nothing to do with the temperature and everything to do with the woman who'd taken up shop in the newly renovated building that sat directly in his line of vision.

A new sign, just delivered and installed that afternoon, sat out front of the green and white building that had once been home to the Senior Ladies' group, all of whom had been Deanie's most loyal customers. They'd shown their support of the town's only female mechanic by pooling their money and helping to fund Romeo's newest business.

He eyed the sign, white like the building, with big green letters that read Deanie's Auto Repair.

He tipped his cowboy hat back and searched for a glimpse of the owner the way he'd done every day for the past two weeks since Valentine's Day and their twenty-four hour interlude.

The longest two weeks of Rance's life.

He wanted her so damned much that his first instinct when he'd heard she'd come home was to drive over to her place, hitch her over his shoulder, take her into the house and love her until she trusted him as much as she loved him.

That was the key ingredient they were missing. While she loved him, she didn't trust him enough to believe that he really loved her.

She knew he lusted after her, and taking her to bed would just prove it.

So he'd kept his distance and bided his time, busying himself with the renovation on the old rodeo arena and hoping like hell she came to her senses. He'd been sleeping on a cot in the main office, putting off actually finding a place of his own until she came around.

But he'd just about reached his limit.

He spotted her through the window that led to the office of her shop and his heart skipped its next beat. As if she sensed his presence, she turned and caught his stare through the window.

It took everything Rance had not to cross the street, but he kept his boots rooted to the pavement and tipped his hat instead. He wasn't going to screw this up by rushing in and bullying her the way she'd done him so many times in the past when they'd been kids.

Rance had something a damned sight different in mind. Something romantic. Something a woman like Deanie Codge wouldn't be able to resist.

At least that's what he told himself. He could only hope like hell that he was right.

DEANIE STOOD in the massive garage that had once hosted bingo parties and Friday afternoon lunches and blinked. Once, twice, but they didn't disappear.

They, as in flowers. Red roses, to be exact. Everywhere she looked. They sat in vases in the corners and on the machinery she'd recently purchased thanks to the senior ladies and a small bank loan. There were roses on the wall-to-wall toolboxes. Her refurbished hydraulic lift. They sat in front of her mountain of oil cans and her computerized transmission test unit.

"Happy Valentine's Day." The deep husky voice

drew her attention to the doorway that led from a small office area to the garage.

She turned to find Rance standing not more than two feet away. He wore faded jeans, a white T-shirt and dusty boots, and he looked every bit the real cowboy now that he'd come home.

She blinked to make sure it was really him because she'd imagined him there too many times over the past two weeks to actually believe it.

But he didn't disappear this time.

She'd seen him around town, but he'd kept his distance and so she'd kept hers, concluding that it had been exactly what she'd feared. Lust, not love. At least on his part, and now it was over.

Finit.

Th-that's all folks!

But now that she saw him up close, she wasn't so sure. He didn't look anything like a man who'd moved on to bigger and better things.

"You look terrible." She noted the taut lines around his mouth and the dark shadows beneath his eyes, as if he hadn't slept in weeks.

Two weeks, to be exact.

"And you look good enough to eat." His gaze roamed her from head to toe, pausing at all the interesting spots in between.

As if she were standing there wearing a sexy teddy rather than old, faded navy blue overalls, her hair pulled up beneath a baseball cap.

As if.

Even as the doubt rolled through her mind, it didn't stir her insecurity. Because Deanie hadn't just come home two weeks ago. She'd come to the realization that she actually liked herself. She wasn't perfect and pretty and sexy like a lot of other women, but that was okay. Being all of those things didn't guarantee success when it came to relationships—Savannah Sierra Ellington had shown her that much.

Likewise, Mavoreen had shown her that a woman didn't have to be any of those things to be wildly successful.

The key, Deanie had come to realize, was being happy with who you were. Content.

Deanie was both of those things now that she'd come back to her element. And she was no longer willing to accept a man who couldn't see beyond her rough exterior. She wanted one who appreciated the fact that she had a wrench and knew how to use it as much as he appreciated the size of her breasts or the length of her legs.

A man who looked at her with his whiskey-colored eyes as if he wanted to eat her up right then and there.

A man who would send her flowers—a whole garage full of them—for Valentine's Day.

She frowned. "It's not Valentine's Day."

"Not technically. But I was hoping we could still celebrate." He crossed the distance to her and handed her a heart made out of red construction paper. "Will you be my valentine?" Before she could reply, he shook his head. "To hell with that." His gaze grew fierce. "I love you, Deanie, and I want you to be a helluva lot more than my valentine. I want you to be my wife."

She stared down at the heart she held in her hands before lifting her gaze to the man who'd held her heart in his for so many years.

And still did.

"I think I can arrange that." And then she threw herself into his arms and kissed him for all she was worth.

* * * * *

And the fling isn't over yet.
Don't miss what else can happen in 24 HOURS in WHEN SHE WAS BAD... by Cara Summers, available next month.

You always want what you don't have

Dinah and Dottie are two sisters who grew up in an imperfect world. Once old enough to make decisions for themselves, they went their separate ways—permanently. Until now. Will their reunion seventeen years later during a series of crises finally help them create a perfect life?

My Perfectly Imperfect Life

Jennifer Archer

HARLEQUIN® *Blaze*

**Follow the twists, turns
and red-hot romances in...**

THE WHITE STAR

ANGELS AND OUTLAWS by Lori Wilde,
Book #230, January 2006

HIDDEN GEMS by Carrie Alexander,
Book #236, February 2006

CAUGHT by Kristin Hardy,
Book #242, March 2006

INTO TEMPTATION by Jeanie London,
Book #248, April 2006

FULL CIRCLE by Shannon Hollis,
Book #254, May 2006

DESTINY'S HAND by Lori Wilde,
Book #260, June 2006

*This modern-day hunt is like no other...
Get your copy today!*

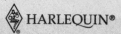

HARLEQUIN®
Blaze™

COMING NEXT MONTH

#237 ONCE UPON A SEDUCTION Jamie Sobrato
It's All About Attitude

He's *so* not Prince Charming. Otherwise Nico Valetti wouldn't be causing all these problems for Skye Ellison. Not the least of which is the fact that she can't keep her hands off him. And since she is traveling in a car with him for days on end, seducing him will just be a matter of time.

#238 BASIC TRAINING Julie Miller

Marine Corps captain Travis McCormick can't believe it when Tess Bartlett—his best friend and new physiotherapist—asks for basic training in sex. Now that he's back in his hometown to recover from injuries, all he wants is a little R & R. Only, Tess has been working on a battle plan for years, and it's time to put it to work. She'll heal him...if he'll make *her* feel all better!

#239 WHEN SHE WAS BAD... Cara Summers
24 Hours: Island Fling, Bk. 3

P.I. Pepper Rossi had no intention of indulging in an island fling. She's at the romantic island resort simply to track down a priceless stolen painting. Only, with sexy ex-CIA agent Cole Buchanan dogging her every step, all she can think about is getting him off her trail...and into her bed!

#240 UP ALL NIGHT Joanne Rock
The Wrong Bed

Devon Baines can't resist the not-so-innocent e-mail invitation. And once he spies Jenny Moore wearing just a little bit of lace, he doesn't care that he wasn't the intended recipient. Sparks fly when these two insomniacs keep company after midnight!

#241 NO REGRETS Cindi Myers

A near-death experience has given her a new appreciation of life. As a result, Lexie Foster compiles a list of things not to be put off any longer. The first thing on her list? An affair with her brand-new boss, Nick Delaney. And convincing him will be half the fun.

#242 CAUGHT Kristin Hardy
The White Star, Bk. 3

With no "out" and no means to reach the outside world, Julia Covington and Alex Spencer are well and truly caught! Trapped in a New York City antiquities museum by a rogue thief isn't the way either one anticipated spending the weekend, but now that it's happened... What will become of the stolen White Star, the charmed amulet Julia is meant to be researching? And what *won't* they do to amuse one another as the hours tick by?

www.eHarlequin.com

HBCNM0206